Snares, Traps, and How to

"Escape Tips from the Smartest Guy Ever"

• Journal Number One •

Joe S. Castillo
Best Selling Author & Artist

Snares, Traps, and How to

Escape!

"Escape Tips from the Smartest Guy Ever"

• Journal Number One •

Joe S. Castillo
Best Selling Author & Artist

Escape! Journal One

© 2023 by Joe S. Castillo

Published by ArtStone Publishers, LLC

International Standard Book Numbers
Hardcover: 978-0-9840459-3-8
Paperback: 978-0-9840459-1-4
eBook: 978-0-9840459-2-1

Library of Congress Number: 2023913190

Cover Design and Illustrations: Joe Castillo

Scripture quotations in the text have been translated, modified from the original Hebrew, and taken from the Free Bible Version. I have taken the liberty of changing some of the wording to fit the narration style of my characters.

The Free Bible Version, though copyrighted, is made available to all under a Creative Commons Attribution-Share Alike (BY-SA) 4.0 International license which allows use and redistribution as long as it is identified as the Free Bible Version, any changes are identified, and derivatives are issued with the same license as the original.

Scripture quotations taken from The Holy Bible, New International Version® NIV® Copyright © 1973, 1978, 1984, 2011 by Biblica, Inc. Used with permission. All rights reserved worldwide.

Printed in the United States

For information on special discounts, bulk purchases, and live programs, contact:

ArtStone Publishers
info@joecastillo.com

Good words from **Escape!** *fans:*

"Authored by my friend Joe Castillo, Escape! is an exciting adventure novel set in Germany during the dark days of the late 1930s. Filled with heart, humor, and wisdom from the book of Proverbs, this is the story of two boys, their grandfather, and a young girl, employing a series of ingenious schemes—and the timely aid of others—to evade capture in an inspiring effort to escape to neighboring Holland."

Dan T. Cathy - Chairman, Chick-fil-A, Inc.

"Young men are regularly tripped up in the same ways. Solomon gave practical advice on how to break the pattern. This exciting story follows two brothers through 1939 Germany, pursued by the military police. The boys are continually rescued by their MacGyver-like, Proverbs-quoting grandfather, Opa. ESCAPE! is a fun adventure story that will inspire boys today."

Bob Goff - Author

"Young boys today face the same traps, snares and temptations they have always faced. Nazi Germany was no different. Joe Castillo has captured the essence of the warnings, escapes, and wisdom given to us by Solomon in the book of Proverbs. He has woven these into a great story that will captivate and inspire young boys today."

Andrew T. Cathy - CEO, Chick-fil-A, Inc.

"My 12 years of involvement with Boys Clubs of America brought to my attention the great need for boys and young men to learn from words of Scripture. The book of Proverbs woven through this engaging story is valuable wisdom for the youth of today."

Rob Parker – President, Trilith Development, LLC

"Escape is a fun read for all ages—a thrilling journey and MacGyver adventure rolled into one. The boys in the story absorb amazing amounts of information from their grandfather, Opa. I know young men who read this book will learn much about life, faith, and character."

Mike Meyer - Delta Pilot, Aviation Instructor

Warning!

Don't get trapped!

Warnings are included with almost every device, tool, toy, food, and package in our world today. We hardly ever read them. Some are silly but we should never forget that real dangers do exist. Many of these dangers have no warning on them. They are designed to trick you into buying an item you don't need and can't afford. Traps will get you signed up for something you should not be part of, or to watch videos that poison your mind.

Nefarious schemes are being invented every minute to entice you to set images before your eyes, allow sounds in your ears, swallow a pill, or invite longings into your heart that can become addictions which in the end will destroy the goodness of life.

Some "snares" can even lead to death.

But … we are never to live our lives in fear. For every "snare and trap" devised, there is a way out. Every wicked plan can be foiled. All devious machinations, pitfalls, and ambushes have a way of escape.

Hundreds of years ago, a brilliant man set out deliberately to examine, explore, and experience many of these "snares and traps." He wrote about what he discovered; his mistakes, bad choices, the pits he fell into, and the tragedies that followed. In his writings he warned about the dangers of these devious devices and how to avoid them. If we are wise and listen to him, we will not be deceived and captured by these "snares and traps."

The book of warnings is called *Proverbs*. Many have read, studied, and memorized parts or all of it. *Escape!* tells the story of one who did and how he did it.

Henry Gutmann - 1946

CHARACTERS

Setting: Germany 1939, just before the Second World War

Grandfather: Alvase Gutmann, called Opa

Henry Gutmann: 15-year-old boy

Hans Gutmann: Henry's 12-year-old brother

Hannah Weis: 15-year-old Jewish girl

The Commandant: Head of Munster SS Military Police

Vilka: German girl in Munster who works in a bookstore

Gretel: Vilka's mother who lives in Osnabrück, Germany

Oskar: Gretel's husband

Duchess Hildegard von Bismarck: Lives in Osnabrück

Zigfried (Zig): A friendly Jewish farmer

Anna: Zig's aunt

Contents

Escape One

"Wise is better than Strong"

The Journal of Henry Gutmann
Munster, Germany - September 1939

I really thought we were going to die.

Two massive Gestapo agents spotted us and shouted, yelling at us to STOP! We didn't. Bullets started flying around us that sounded like angry bees whizzing by. All of the Jews in Germany were being rounded up and sent to concentration camps. We were not Jewish, but anyone who helped Jews was also in trouble. My parents had been taken away two weeks ago just for being kind to our Jewish neighbors. My Grandfather 'Opa' found my brother and me locked in a secret attic room. After four days without food, we were starving. That was the first time he saved our lives.

I have to tell you more about 'Opa,' or Oompah. We called him that sometimes because he used to play the tuba in a polka band. He could build anything, play music with a blade of grass, and still walk on his hands even though he was seventy years old. Most of all, he knew how to be wise and clever. The many jobs he had worked in his life taught him about machines, locks, explosives, and any kind of gadget you could find in various stores. Bags of bits, parts, and other leftovers of these gadgets always filled his pockets. His most prized possession, a handy Swiss Army Knife, remained strapped on his belt. It contained eighteen

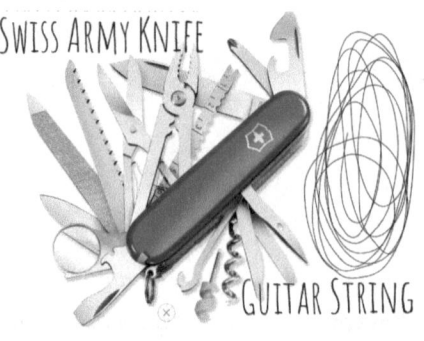

SWISS ARMY KNIFE

GUITAR STRING

tools in one: needle nose pliers, a pair of wire cutters, a knife, a saw blade, a file, an awl, a can opener, a bottle opener, scissors, tweezers, a toothpick, a lockpick, a magnifying glass, a tiny hammer, and four different screwdrivers. He could fix anything with it. His most impressive ability was not visible. At the age of thirteen he had memorized the entire book of Proverbs and could still recite it all. We heard pieces of it all the time. He could also make us laugh. But we weren't laughing now. I knew we were going to die.

"Keep your heads down, boys, and run! *'Evil people hide, but they ambush only themselves!'*"

Down a flight of steps, then we turned and fled under a stone bridge that formed a tunnel beneath the road overhead. We raced along a narrow dock with the heavy sound of boots clumping down the stairs behind us. As we ran, my grandfather pulled some things from the giant pockets in his coat. We turned another corner. A spool of wire and the pliers of his Swiss Army Knife appeared in his hands. He suddenly stopped, stooped down, and wrapped one end of the wire around a cleat on the dock and the other around a metal post. Stretched across the path at knee height, the wire—so fine in the gloom—became invisible. A quick twist and clip with the pliers, then he jumped up, running again.

Steps climbed on the other side of the tunnel which led up to the street ahead. We didn't even hesitate. Behind us, the running footsteps of the two heavy guards were abruptly stilled by a high-pitched twang, a series of loud thumps, a crash, and twin splashes from the canal. Opa chuckled. "Here, boys, follow me." Running up, out, and back across the bridge at street level, he then turned onto the steps we had already run down. We were going in a circle! Why would we go right back down to where we had just been running from the guards? But I knew better than to question Opa. He had bailed us out of so many tight spots, I knew he had a plan. We stopped at the bottom of the stairs and peeked around the corner. We could not see the soldiers, but we could hear them splashing and cursing as they dragged themselves out of the canal.

"If I get my hands on that old man and his two idiot kids, I am going to peel them like a rutabaga," one of them said. The other one answered, "Well, the Commandant is going to peel us like rutabagas. We not only let them escape but we lost our rifles in the water and how do we explain that?" With a lot of sloshing and stomping, their voices faded as they climbed the stairs at the other end of the tunnel. The three of us walked silently back to the spot where Opa's wire had tripped them up. He mimicked one of the soldiers tripping and falling in the water. Hans and I laughed quietly.

"Don't worry, boys," he said as he bent down to retrieve his wire. With a chuckle, he continued, "those two dunces would never dream that we would double back around and return to the scene of the crime." He sat down on the dock and waved to us to sit as he coiled up the wire and placed it back in a pocket. "That simple guitar string played a nice tune." With a grin, he pulled a bag from another pocket. Black bread and cream cheese came out of the bag for a late evening snack. "You see, boys, *'A wise person can take on armed soldiers and their weapons will fall.'* So it says in the best book of wisdom in the whole world. He that inspired it also says of those who reject him, *'He will laugh when disaster strikes them and make fun when calamity overtakes them.'*" Opa threw back his head and laughed. Way louder than I thought safe. So in the semi-darkness of the stone tunnel, we sat, ate our black bread and cheese, and planned out what we would do next.

I had started keeping notes about these adventures so I could write about them later. If we got captured or killed, somebody might find this journal and know how many times God rescued us. I guess in the end, if He doesn't, I might have to write about that too—if I live through it! They would also know what a wise and clever man Grandfather was. It would tell them where he got his wisdom and how it saved us over and over again.

My name is Henry Gutmann. I am fifteen and Hans, my brother, is three years younger, but he always was the winner, in sports, school, and even when competing in games. He was even bigger and stronger so he pretended to be the older one. Twelve is a hard age. You start thinking you know everything, but you don't. Fifteen is even harder. Especially when we grew up in a nice home, went to a wonderful school with lots of friends, and suddenly it's all gone. Hans and I had lost our parents and it seemed like we had lost everything else too. On top of that, we were hiding from the Gestapo. We were terrified, with no idea what to do.

In the middle of all this hardship, our grandfather had shown up. My Grandmother Molly had died not too many years ago, so he lived alone, but he was a superhero to us. Clearly Grandfather's life showed that *"It is better to be wise than strong. Smarts win out over muscle every time."* I identified with him because he was not big or strong, but we had seen him for as many years as I can remember, quietly, cheerfully, and patiently going about doing wise things. One of his favorite sayings was "If you are going to be dumb, you better be tough," but more important, *"Whoever listens to wisdom will live in safety and be at ease, without fear of harm."*

I also have to tell you about The Commandant who became our sworn enemy. I added this part of the story later when we actually met him and I found out why he became obsessed with trying to catch us.

We didn't die that night. But it began a series of adventures that I would not believe were true if I had not lived them. Keep reading. You might not believe it either or that my grandfather rescued us again. This time with hair clippers, two fake uniforms, and some hollow books. First you need to know where the adventures began.

The Commandant was not happy. Actually, he was furious! Standing before him, the two wet soldiers shivered while he ranted, cursed, threatened, and whacked his desk with his metal walking stick. Towering behind that desk, the soldiers were afraid they were going to get hit next. "You idiots! You allowed a senile old man and two children to escape! You are soldiers of the Third Reich. You are strong. You are mighty. You cannot be made into fools! You must, you will prevail, or the full force of the Führer will come down upon you!"

Escape Two

"Right is better than Wrong"

The Journal of Henry Gutmann
Claudiospatz Street, Munster, Germany - August 1939

"Be absolutely silent," my mother whispered. "Do not move from here until we return to get you. There is no safety out on the streets." Father stood behind her in the shadows. We could hear loud banging on the front door. Commands shouted by gruff voices floated up to the attic. Then, mother sealed us in the secret cabinet. Their footsteps shuffled down the winding stairs and we didn't see them again. Four days in total darkness. Four days without food. Four days with only the gallon of water they had left with us, and the bucket we had to pee into. I couldn't open the secret door. It was locked from the outside. We tried kicking the door open until our feet hurt, but solid oak was not going to break. When we weren't sleeping, I cried silently most of the time. I know Hans could feel my back shaking as we leaned against each other for support. Hans held the tears in, trying to be tough. I knew nobody would ever find us. We would starve to death.

Most people wouldn't understand the danger we were living under except our grandfather, Opa. In class, Hans and I had been pressured to join Hitler's Youth. If you did, you got lots of cool things. First, a very nice uniform with a red neckerchief you could wear to school. Field trips, parties, and days out of class for special rallies made everyone not in the group envious.

"You must not join them," Opa told us. "Boys, the wisdom of the Good Book tells you, *'Do not join with them, don't even walk with them; for their feet rush into evil, they are quick to shed blood.'*"

Later we discovered what he said was true. Some of the kids who had been our best friends joined and right away started spying on their parents and their neighbors. Many Jews were ratted out and sent to the prison camps because of Hitler's Youth. Fredrick, one of our school friends, lived across the street. When he joined up, he would make fun of us and say that we were traitors to the Reich. He probably spied on my parents and saw them helping the Jews escape. I am almost sure that his information caused my parents to be taken away. He must have seen them taking Jews in, but he could not have known of the secret room in our attic. Nobody knew about that. Now we were locked in it. It would be a slow death.

But Opa came. He had followed my parents and the long line of captives as they were herded to a barbed wire containment area. For three days he searched the crowded camp. On the fourth day he spotted my tall father and frail mother in a corner.

"The boys," she croaked to him. "The boys are locked in the attic."

"Never lose hope," whispered Opa to them, *"for the hope of the righteous brings joy."*

It was all he got to say before cruel guards began shoving them toward the railway cars that would take them to the death camps.

Hans and I were stuffing fruit and smoked mackerel on black bread sandwiches into our starving bellies as Grandfather told us how he had escaped the deportation.

"I know you are hungry, boys, yet it is better to eat slowly."

"It's never rude to eat food," spoke Hans, who had a knack for rhyming his words.

"Ah," Opa said with a smile. "A fake heart attack and fall. It was easy to convince the guards that I was dead, lying face first in a deep mud puddle. You can't breathe underwater. What they could not see was a clear plastic tube running behind my ear into my old hat. I breathed through it just fine."

But he had to lie there in the mud for more than an hour until a body collector came by with a push wagon, loaded him up, wheeled him outside the fence, and dumped him down a steep slope into a trench dug for dead bodies. Opa chuckled.

"I lay real still and pretended to be dead until midnight when I could sneak away. *'The path of life leads upward for the wise; they leave the grave behind,'*" he quoted. "Another young man with a bloody wound on his head pretended to be dead as well. I bandaged him up and sent him off to see if he could find his family." My grandfather shook his head with a rare look of grief on his face. "I think they were loaded on the train along with your parents. Very sad."

"But Opa," I said, "you don't look all muddy and you are wearing nice, clean clothes. How did that happen?"

With his blue eyes all crinkled up, he laughed out loud.

"'*He gives good judgment to those who live right.*' The "janitor" at the mineral springs spa on Velstrasse can take a bath and pick some clean clothes from the left-behind bin at the end of his shift." Add janitor, another job Grandfather worked, to the list I did not know about.

"How did you find us in the secret room?" The muffled question came from Hans, around a bite of sandwich. Reaching into yet another of his large pockets, out came a stethoscope, like the kind doctors use.

"Opa, did you ever work as a doctor?" I asked.

"Yah, a medic in the first war. It still works. I could hear you breathing behind the hidden panel. Once I knew where you were, I figured out how to open the latch easily. Look here." He pointed to the latch on the door. "If you knew, you could have let yourselves out, '*So let the wise listen and add to their learning.*'"

Hans asked a much harder question. "If we had not been helping the Jews ..." His lips tightened. "They would not have taken Mom and Dad." Suddenly angry he continued, "Why would they do that? They should have let the Jews be taken away!" I nodded in agreement. A lump rose in my throat, tears puddled in my eyes.

"No, boys," Opa answered with real sternness in his voice. "We know what the Nazis have done is wicked, but you cannot think that way. We should never find a 'good' reason for ignoring evil. For we have been told by God himself to *'Rescue those who are being dragged off to die; save them as they stagger to their death.'* You can't make excuses by saying, *'We didn't know what was going on,'* because God knows everything you are thinking. He even sees your soul and knows what is in it. *'He will reward everybody for what they did.'* He will punish the evil and reward the good."

I just lowered my head and shook it from side to side. That was hard to take.

"Well," he announced cheerfully, "finish up and change into … these!" Proudly, he held up two brand new Hitler Youth uniforms.

"What?!" Hans almost spit. "I won't wear those things! I don't give a hoot, I won't wear that monkey suit." Hans loved words. He read lots of books and always made up his own poems.

Opa snorted a laugh. "Yah, you can, Hans. The best disguise is to look exactly like the enemy."

"But why, Opa?" I knew as I asked that his answer would be, as always, short and to the point.

"We are in Munster, still far from Netherlands, but there is much danger here. We have to get out of Germany for safety. So a disguise is necessary."

A new device popped out of Opa's coat. Hand hair clippers. Both Hans and I had let our hair grow longer in a silent rebellion against the Hitler Youth. They wore their hair cut close on the sides and spiky on top. Now Opa, starting with Hans, cut our hair to match. I guess it made sense. By the time he was done we looked like poster boys for the Nazi Führer.

Hans did not look happy.

Dawn started creeping in the window.

"Step quickly, boys. I am your grandfather, taking you to school." We pushed our old clothes and leftover trash into the hidden room and latched the secret door. Opa carried a canvas rucksack. Hans led the way, Opa behind him. Fearful of leaving the safety of the house, I lagged back.

Grandfather looked back, encouraging me, *"The Lord is a shield to those whose walk is blameless. He guards the path of the just and protects the way of his faithful ones."*

Out on the street, on a Monday morning, people seemed to be going about their work as normal. We lived in one of the nice houses on Claudiospatz Street, but we were walking away from downtown Munster on Hanauer Strasse toward the train station. One obvious difference was the stores and shops that had been owned by the Jews were closed. Large painted Stars of David had been scrawled on their storefronts and windows. There were also many armed policemen and soldiers carrying guns. Walking down the sidewalk with the crowd, Opa steered us along until we reached a bookshop on the corner. The bell over the door rang as we walked in. At the counter near the front, a young woman looked up and smiled as she saw Opa, but her face changed to a stiff mask when she saw us boys.

"Heil Hitler," Grandfather said with a very small snicker in his voice. "Peace, Vilka, no need for anxiety. These are my grandsons. They are dressed for a play." He grinned. "The biggest part they may ever play in their young lives. You have some books for us, yah?"

The young girl seemed to relax when she understood that we were just wearing disguises, even though Hans looked very uncomfortable. She reached into a closet behind her.

"Boys, you need to know well who will open their mouths and who can keep them closed. Vilka and her family are trustworthy friends. It tells us in The Book, '*A gossip betrays a confidence, but a trustworthy person keeps a secret.*'"

Returning, the girl handed each of us a couple of books. They all looked like the textbooks we used for school. Two of them were a set of encyclopedias by Funk and Wagnalls. With a nod from Opa, we walked all the way to a worktable in the back of the store where he laid the books flat and opened to the first few pages. From his rucksack, he removed a number of devices that looked like miniature power tools and laid them on top of the opened books. With a black marker he traced each tool and, using an electric jigsaw, cut out the shape of the tool and set each book aside. We watched nervously. Books were expensive and we had always been taught to take care of them.

"Come take a look, things hidden in a book," rhymed Hans. I couldn't help squinting my eyes shut and shaking my head.

Ever since he had started learning about poetry in school, he fancied himself a poet.

Reaching under the counter, Opa pulled out a bottle of bookbinder's cement and spread it on the inside of the shape he had cut. By the time he finished, the glue on the first book had dried. The very last book was bigger. In it he had cut the shape of a gun. Faster than I could imagine, he had placed each tool in its exact opening, made two stacks, and wrapped each stack in a leather belt. Three books in a stack, a bit heavier than regular books, but they looked like ordinary school books. Hans and I looked exactly like school kids on our way to class. The last book, the one with the gun, Opa tucked under his arm. As we left the shop, a knowing glance passed between him and the shopkeeper. A silent thank you. It was a look of hope.

We had no sooner walked out of the store when the next adventure began. It involved a Dremel tool, two pinch clips, and a map of Germany.

In a grey, windowless office, the Commandant quivered with pent-up tension. Pressed against the side of his bullet-shaped head, covering one of his small peanut-shaped ears, was the black phone receiver. Mouth slit, jaw clenched, forehead flushed red. The words coming from the phone were obviously not pleasant. But under black eyebrows, his beady eyes set too close to his crooked nose showed anger. "Yah, General, we know exactly

where he is," he lied. "I do not believe him to be a spy. If he is, the boys are just a cover. We will have him in custody today and we will squeeze him until he confesses everything. There is no hope for him." The Commandant knew if he did not follow through and catch the old man there was no hope for himself either.

#

"STRAIGHT IS BETTER THAN CROOKED"

The Journal of Henry Gutmann
On the road out of Munster, Germany - September 1939

Only if you have lived in a country where the rulers have become totally evil can you understand how scary it is to try and live a normal life. My family never worried about the police, or prison camps, or doing things that were against the law. Learning about right and wrong was an important part of what they taught us. I remember at six years old I had taken a toy car from a store without paying for it, and my father very gently explained that I had done wrong. He made me return to the store, give the toy back to the manager, and tell him with tears running down my face that I had taken the toy and I was sorry.

I could even remember what Opa had said. *"Trust in the Lord and do what is right. In everything you do submit to Him and He will keep you on the straight path."* Hans and I had learned that stealing, lying, killing, disrespecting our parents, and wanting what we should not have was wrong.

It seemed so sudden when the people in our government began doing ALL those things. Regularly, without shame, they began punishing those who pointed it out. I remember the day at school we were told that Hitler, the new leader of our country, the self-appointed Führer, was never wrong. The teacher was never wrong. The principal was never wrong. If we questioned their leadership or authority we were immediately subjected to punishment. Five lashes with a cane, usually. The world we lived in suddenly became terribly crooked.

Main Street was busy. Trucks, buses, and cars were roaring by, but too many of the vehicles were military and Gestapo, the Nazi police force. I knew we were in danger of being spotted as undesirables but Grandfather strolled along enjoying the best day of his life. That was how he lived. Every day was a good day, even if you were in danger of being arrested, interrogated, and sent to a prison camp any minute. Up ahead he noticed a clump of people being detained by the Gestapo.

They were examining peoples' papers, their credentials. We had no papers. To turn around and run now would be a dead giveaway that we didn't want to be questioned and show our papers. Standing to one side, the obvious leader was the Commandant. His stone-cold black eyes, too close to his crooked nose, watched everything. For a second his beady eyes locked onto mine, freezing me with fear. A tug from Opa's hand pulled me off the curb and moved us behind a large panel truck.

"Come, boys." With a simple motion, he opened the back door of the truck and helped us in. "We will catch a ride to our destination." When he closed the door, it went pitch black, but the gleam of the Commandant's piercing eyes and the evil that lay behind them remained glowing in my brain. I would never forget that look.

A rustling sound produced a bright light. Holding a flat round disk up high, Opa set the flashlight against the wall of the truck and with a metallic click the magnet on the back stuck it to the wall. Perfect, we could see everything.

"Help me, boys," Grandfather whispered, as he began moving boxes around until we had created a space where we could hide. With his Swiss Army Knife, he quickly cut one box open, emptied it, and set it above us so that inside, the truck looked like it held nothing but stacked boxes. Detaching his light, we sat in the dark. None too soon. The door opened, more boxes were loaded, the door slammed shut, and the truck started to move.

We had only traveled a short distance when we began to hear the shouts of the Gestapo. "Stop! What do you have in there?" The truck stopped and the door opened again.

"Only tools. It is just tools and supplies for the munitions factory," whined the driver. The sound of boots climbing in the back made me shiver. This was it! We were doomed. A few boxes got shoved around. Some were opened. Boots clumped off the back and the door slammed shut. With that, the truck moved off again and we all breathed a sigh of relief.

"Well, well. Tools," chuckled my Opa excitedly. "You can never have too many tools," he said with enthusiasm. The flashlight went up again and we started rummaging around in the boxes. Every box got opened and it seemed as if Grandfather memorized what each one contained. We rattled along a city road until we turned onto a smooth highway. Most of the boxes carried tools that were too heavy for us to use, but Opa did pocket some items. He pulled out of one pocket what looked like a compact sewing kit.

"Opa, do you really know what you are doing?" muttered Hans. "This whole thing seems dumb, we don't know where we are going or where we came from." I was embarrassed. Hans should not be telling Opa he was dumb. I knew he had not spent as much time with him, and Hans sometimes gave my parents a hard time.

"Hans, don't say things like that. He knows exactly what he's doing. And you do know where we're going, don't you, Opa?"

"Well, not exactly, boys. We are going straight instead of crooked, but it would help to know if we are going in the right direction." Sliding a needle from the kit, he rubbed it back and forth on a bit of silk cloth and attached it to a fine thread. "This will show us which way we are going. I have created a magnet by rubbing this steel needle on silk. Magnets are such wonderful things. Now you know how to make a compass." Holding the needle up to the light, its shadow cast on the lid of a white box quivered and turned, pointing toward the back of the truck. "Ah." Opa sounded disappointed. "We are going south. Probably headed for Munich toward the prison camps. We should be going north to get to Denmark or west toward Holland. If we keep going this way, we will never get out of Germany. We must fix that."

Reaching into another deep pocket, out came a strange tool I had never seen before.

"This is a battery-run Dremel. Like a drill, you can put all sorts of tips on it." The floor of the truck was made up of metal panels, held down with Phillips head screws. "Here, Hans. Start taking screws out of this panel here. This button turns it on. This switch makes it go forward and this one backward. Set it on backward to take out the screws. Always remember, "lefty-loosey ... righty-tighty. Henry, you start moving these boxes so we can lift the panel and get to the fuel line." Hans quickly learned how to use the Dremel, and soon the metal plate came loose and Opa lifted one edge. It was terrifying! You could see the road flying by. The driveshaft was spinning. Heat came radiating off the exhaust pipe. Bits of dirt and dust flew

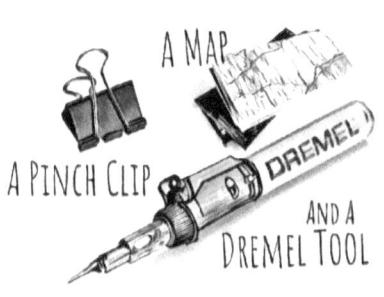

A MAP

A PINCH CLIP

DREMEL

AND A
DREMEL TOOL

into our faces. But with a quick move, like a magician, Opa pulled a spring clamp from his coat. He located and pinched a rubber hose that ran up toward the engine. "Quick, put everything back, but Hans, only put in a couple of screws. We will need to get back in here soon. We sat again in the dark. Within minutes, the truck engine sputtered, stopped, then silence. The back door opened. Muttering. Cursing. Still we sat quiet. Another vehicle stopped beside the truck. Muffled, we could hear the voice complain, "I know I could not have run out of gas, but the engine instantly quit. Could you give me a ride back to Munster? I am just a driver. I need a mechanic."

"Sure, no problem. Hop in." Before the sound of the other car had faded away, we were pulling up the panel, removing the clip and replacing the screws. Hans was getting to be a pro with the Dremel.

"Now let's get out of here." Moving toward the back doors, Grandfather talked as if he were thinking out loud. "This door is latched from the outside. We are locked in." All this was said not like it was a serious problem but just our next puzzle to solve. "I think the Dremel will work again here." Taking it from Hans, he replaced the Phillips head screwdriver tip with a standard flat tip since the screws were basic slot head screws.

"Three ways of opening a locked door. One, pick the lock. We can't do that because the lock is outside. Two, remove the hinge pins. We can't do that because the pins are outside also. Three, remove the hinges. So let us do that. Here, Henry, you can do this, but do it quickly." Opa moved the magnetic light close to the hinge and I started removing the screws. In less time than I thought possible, the door started sagging open and with the removal of the last screw, fell out onto the street.

"Bolt cutters," called Grandfather, standing on the tailgate of the truck. "Conveniently packed in one of the boxes, this tool will cut through any lock made." After lifting the two doors up, Opa handed me what looked like a giant pair of pliers with sharp teeth. Sure enough, it cut through the metal lock like cheese.

"Wow, Opa. What else can you cut with these?"

"Most amazing invention, these bolt cutters. You can cut chains, cables, heavy wire, and, of course, locks." One by one, the doors were screwed back into place and we were ready to roll. It was high noon outside, so the magnetic light had been replaced with a map of Germany from one of Grandfather's pockets. He walked toward the driver's side of the truck and opened the door.

"Nice that he left this unlocked, but alas, he did not leave the keys in the ignition. Not a big problem. Look, here under the dashboard." He pointed to some wires under the steering wheel. "Hot wiring can be easy in these ancient trucks. Three wires. A black wire, a white wire, and a blue one." He unfolded the wire snips from his Swiss Army Knife, then snipped and stripped all three wires. "Blue and white get twisted together. Touch the black one to the other two and presto, the starter turns over. It takes a bit longer to start than usual, because it needs to pull gas all the way from where we had it clamped." Soon enough the engine roared to life and we all piled into the cab. "Now we are going to borrow this nice man's truck and it will take us straight to where we need to go." The map unfolded and I traced the red lines across to our hometown of Munster.

"Opa, I think we are lost. How can we find out where we are?" asked Hans.

"The road signs will tell us soon, but I do know we need to turn around since we were going the wrong way. We were going south, toward Munich, where we surely would be caught. We need to go north toward Osnabrück, then on to Holland, which is a long way.

"But Opa, do we know where they have taken our parents?" I spoke with a catch in my throat, feeling like at any moment I might cry again. "Should we not be looking for them?"

"I'm sorry, Henry. We have no idea where they've been taken and I must get you two to safety. Also, we have friends in Osnabrück. They can help us." The truck pulled forward and soon a wide spot in the road allowed Opa to turn around and head the other way. No crooked roads for us.

FOLDING CANE

GLASSES

OLD HAT

"Boys, stay on the straight road. *'Wisdom will save you from the ways of wicked men, from men whose words are crooked, who have left straight paths to walk in dark places, who get excited in being disobedient and rejoice in doing evil things. Their ways are crooked.'* We need to stay on the straight road." Green fields lay on either side of white fences and the sun shone on the road ahead. Humming to himself, Opa murmured, *"The path of the righteous is like the morning sun, shining ever brighter till the full light of day."*

We were making good time. He was content. What we didn't know was that an adventure waited around the next bend in the road and Grandfather would need a folding cane, an old hat, glasses, a come-along pulley, and knowing how to tie some knots.

"What do you mean he disappeared?" yelled the Commandant. "This old man cannot be a master spy. He fooled you. He is crooked and clever. You need to be even more crooked than he is." The five Gestapo soldiers in the room looked nervous. They were shifting their feet and fumbling with their weapons. "He must be just some Jew-loving dolt who is trying to hide from our forces. Or he is a despicable Jew himself. He will not be able to hide his crooked schemes from us. Now go!"

Escape Four

"Confidence is Better than Fear"

The Journal of Henry Gutmann
On the road to Osnabrück, Germany - September 1939

Bang! Crash! Clatter! The truck came to a sudden halt. All the tools in the back smashed forward in the back of the truck. Right in the middle of the road were two grey-green military vehicles along with half a dozen Gestapo soldiers.

"Out! Get out of the truck!" The soldier yelled. Hans and I climbed down from the cab. I looked back and watched Opa as he climbed down from the driver's seat. He had put on a dirty old hat and a pair of thick glasses. A pained expression wrinkled his face and he moved slowly, as if badly crippled. Using a cane that had appeared from somewhere, he limped up to the beefy soldier. Peering up through the thick, dirty lenses, he croaked in a feeble, ancient voice.

"Heil Hitler, Sergeant," he saluted painfully. "What seems to be the problem? My noble grandsons spent the weekend with me and I am dropping them back to school, driving a load of tools to the munitions factory. You can see they are good boys in the Nazi Youth. Fine looking boys, aren't they? Yes, yes, fine boys." He pointed toward us with what looked like a crippled hand.

"What's in the truck, old man?" the sergeant demanded, followed by a string of dirty words. He waved to another soldier. "Private, check out what they are hauling."

"It is tools, Commandant. Tools for the war effort." Grandfather wheezed, out of breath as if from the effort, pointing at the truck with the cane. My blood suddenly turned to ice. The sergeant was taking our books from the front seat. They were all stacked and belted, but I was sure he would unbuckle the strap, open one of them and …

"Careful with the textbooks, Sergeant!" Opa cautioned in his gravelly voice. "You know the schools will charge my grandsons and punish them if they are damaged." The sergeant smiled at my "feeble, old" grandfather and put them gently back on the seat.

"I know, old man, I have three boys of my own."

"Nothing here, Sergeant," the soldier yelled. "Good luck with your studies, boys." The sergeant was not nearly as nice. "Get on out of here. We can't have you blocking the highway." His language was full of words I had heard boys in the Hitler Youth say, but only once had one of those words come out of my mouth at home. It had snapped my mother into action, making me stick out my tongue so she could rub it intensely with a bar of lye soap.

"Never," she made very clear, "will you ever use words like that in this house, young man."

Opa's step clearly changed to a confident, brisk pace as we headed back and climbed into the truck. As soon as we got out of sight of the Gestapo behind us, all three of us started laughing and cheering.

"Yikes, Opa," I murmured. "Mom would have washed his mouth out with soap quick."

"So true, Henry. *'Keep your mouth free of perversity; keep corrupt talk far from your lips.'*"

"I was scared," said Hans, shivering. "We are going to get caught eventually. I know it."

"Ah, don't be afraid, Hans. Remember, confidence is always better than fear. *'Wisdom will protect you, she will watch over you.'*"

"You make a very convincing 'old man,'" I said, laughing. "I know you don't wear glasses. You probably had them in one of your pockets, but where did you get that cane? That is way too big to hide in your coat."

"The glasses do need to come off. I can't see anything through these things. The cane, well, that is easy, easy. Watch this." With one hand, he picked up the cane, pushed a button on the handle and tapped the tip on the floorboard. "Presto!" the cane folded into itself, leaving a short metallic tube he could hide in any pocket. "It makes a fine baton, too, for self-defense."

Accelerating forward, we were on the road back to Munster. Signs on the highway pointing the way, we only had about another forty-five minutes to go. Without warning, Opa turned off the main road.

"We are going to take a detour around Munster, boys, because we don't want anyone to spot our 'borrowed' truck."

For the next twenty kilometers, all went fine, but the road eventually deteriorated into a muddy track. It looked as if it had been bombed by the Allies. Wrestling with the wheel, Grandfather managed to keep the truck moving, but a deep puddle brought us to a complete halt. The wheels bogged down. They spun in the mud. The truck stopped. Only about one hundred yards ahead lay clear, paved highway, but we were not moving an inch. Hans moaned and put his head on the dashboard.

"Not a problem, boys, just another adventure." No longer the feeble old man with the cane, Opa jumped out of the truck and started issuing orders. "Henry, climb into the back and find the box that has the roll of metal cable. It will be heavy. Hans, you are looking for the box that has six winches. We will need at least one."

"I don't know what a winch looks like, Opa."

"Not a problem, Hans. Henry can show you. It is a metal frame with gears, a handle, and a coil of wire in the middle. Some people call it a come-along." I wasn't so sure, but jumped down from the truck right into the puddle and waded toward the back to start looking. Grandfather walked off down the muddy road. Soon we had the roll of cable with a hook at each end and this weird-looking contraption that Grandfather had described. He uncoiled the cable and stretched it across the mud, wrapped it around a solid oak tree, and walked back to where we were. Now wire attached to the come-along connected it to the massive oak tree. Pulling the wire from the come-along behind, he knelt down under the truck.

"Ok, look under here, boys. Every car, truck, tank, or military vehicle made has a utility hook on the frame. If we tried to pull from the bumper, it would rip right off. The hook will hold the entire weight of the truck." With that, he created a loop of wire and slipped it over the hook. "Now, Henry, with the winch you will be strong enough to pull a truck!"

Opa showed me how to start cranking the winch. The spool took up the slack. The cable got tighter with each pull on the handle, the ratchet clicked to keep it from uncoiling and— surprise, surprise—the truck started to 'come along.' Amazing! It took a lot of pulls. We all took turns pulling the handle. The truck kept inching forward until we were totally beyond the mud. After tossing the wire and winch back in the truck, we were on the road again. Opa was very satisfied.

"An amazing tool, the come-along. It gives you the strength of fifty men. We were trapped in the mud but, *'the goodness of those who live right will save them, the dishonest are trapped by their own*

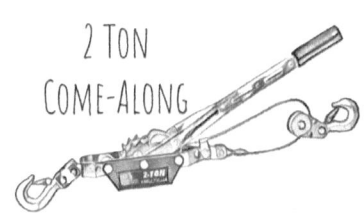

desires.' I have a tiny winch somewhere in my coat, but for a heavy truck loaded down with tools, we needed the big one. Now we need to find some food. I am getting real hungry. How about you boys?"

We knew what it was to be very hungry, so we had not complained, but some food sounded very good. Late in the afternoon, a few kilometers down the road, we spotted a farmhouse nestled in the woods, partially hidden from the road. Opa pulled into the track leading to the house. As we bumped closer, we saw smoke coming from the chimney and could imagine the smell of hot food on a stove. My mouth started to water at the thought. Over to one side we saw two cars that we had not been able to see from the road. The truck stopped beside them and before we climbed out Grandfather cautioned us.

"Be careful now, boys. Bring the books with you and let me do the talking." As he stepped to the front door, it opened abruptly, revealing a tall, skinny man with deep-set eyes and a black bushy eyebrow that ran all the way across his forehead. He looked angry.

"Who are you? What are you doing here? What do you want?" The voice was tense.

"Greetings, Comrade, I am very sorry to disturb you. My grandsons and I are traveling to Munster, but my truck is almost out of petrol. The petrol stations are rare. We were hoping to buy a couple of liters so we could make it to a nearby petrol station."

He spoke casually, without nervousness, and a wide smile on his face. "We would appreciate your kindness tremendously. Running out and spending the night on the road would be hard on the boys."

A frown wrinkled the black eyebrow across the man's face. Stone-still for almost a minute, he obviously had something on his mind. I did notice that he had one hand behind his back. He looked nervous. With a swift move, he backed away and commanded, "Come in." This was a clear command, not an invitation. At that point, Opa put a protective arm around Hans and began backing away.

"Thank you, sir. I sense this to be an imposition ..." But the hidden hand appeared, pointing a very lethal-looking pistol right at Opa's chest. It looked like a German-made Luger.

"I said come in. Do not attempt anything foolish." Opa tightened his grip on Hans's shoulder and, with nowhere to run, he pulled Hans behind him and we stepped into the house. The man backed to one side and slammed the door. "Into the kitchen, quickly." He motioned with the gun. Even though the light was fading as the sun headed for the horizon, I could see two other people in the room. An older couple, both tied to kitchen chairs.

The thin man pulled some coils of rope from the table and tossed them to Opa. "Quick, tie up the boys and don't make any trouble. I will shoot the little one first." Hans went very white. His face mirrored the fear I felt.

Opa did not seem worried at all. He softly said, "Of course, Comrade." We set our books on the table as he pushed Hans into one of the other chairs and reached for the rope. He tied him up. I was next. Yet Opa did not tie the ropes very tightly. As he wrapped the rope around my hands behind my back, he slipped a pocketknife into my hands.

"Now, you!" growled the man. "Sit on the floor here. And no talking." Since all four chairs were now taken, he roughly took the rest of the rope and tied Grandfather up. Hands, arms, and feet. It looked impossible for him to move, much less escape. The man looked over all of our ropes and moved into the front of the house, where we heard him settle down on a couch by the front door.

An oil lamp hung from the ceiling and, by its feeble light, I got a chance to look at the other two people tied up in the kitchen chairs. They were older, about the age of my parents. On a regular day they would have looked like chubby, rosy-cheeked country farmers. Tonight, they were as pale as Hans. They looked terrified. We sat for a long time. My hands were starting to tingle and grow numb. I was afraid I would drop the knife on the floor. Finally, we heard snoring from the front room.

"Greetings, friends," whispered Opa to the elderly couple. "What is going on with our malicious friend?" At first they seemed hesitant to speak. Slowly, the husband whispered, "That is the village mayor. The Gestapo appointed him and he discovered we were helping Jews escape into Holland. In the morning, he intends to take us in to the police station in Munster. I am sure we will get sent to the prison camps." His wife hung her head and I saw a tear roll down her cheek. "It looks like you might be deported with us." I'm sure the couple could not understand why, even in the dim light, Grandfather still had a cheerful smile on his face.

"Perhaps," he whispered. "Perhaps not." Something was going on in his brain, I knew it.

"We are never going to ride until we get untied. So how are we going to escape, Opa?" asked Hans, gloomily.

Like a magician doing an escape trick, Opa flourished the one hand he had already pulled free. A finger to his lips, he made a move that reminded me of a snake I had seen once in a circus. He wriggled out of his ropes and stood up. Quickly he untied the couple and then us. Again, in a whisper, he said, "Sit still and be silent. If I shout, run out the back door and escape in one of the two cars." Moving silently, he unstrapped one of the books on the table and pulled out the gun hidden inside. He winked at the older couple, whose eyes had grown large in fear and amazement. With the gun in one hand and a length of rope in the other, he vanished around the corner into the front room. It was not a surprise to hear the skinny man grunt a flurry of cursing and evil words.

"Oh, be quiet," we heard Opa say cheerfully. "'*The words of the wicked are like a deadly ambush, but there is rescue in the words of the upright.*' Come here, boys, and let me show you how to tie knots that do not come undone so easily." There he stood. He had taken away the man's gun and had already looped some of the rope around his arms and chest.

"This knot here is called a granny knot. Never use a granny knot. Here is how you tie a square knot. This one does not come

untied." With that, and lessons on other more complicated knots, he had Mr. Eyebrow looking like a German sausage. His own handkerchief tied over his mouth kept him quiet.

Not that it made any difference since we were far from the main road.

"Oh yes, Comrade," Grandfather lectured Mr. Eyebrows, *"Your ways are in full view of the Lord. He knows everything you do. Wicked people are trapped by their evil deeds, the ropes of your sins will bind you tight."*

"Thank you, thank you!" said the woman, rubbing her hands on her apron.

"Opa, were you going to shoot him?" I asked.

Throwing his head back to laugh, he answered, "Not a chance. This gun is not loaded and I have no bullets. But, very much like our last kidnapper, fear should never keep you from doing things. *'Don't ever be afraid of people, that will become a trap, but if you trust in the Lord you will be safe.'"*

"Very true, sir," the woman said. "But what can we do to repay you?"

Opa tucked the gun back into its book hideaway and spoke kindly. "There is no debt to repay, lady, but the boys and I have not eaten since breakfast, so if you have a crust of bread and some water it would provide sustenance."

The pink seemed to rise into her cheeks and a smile burst forth.

"Of course. Yah, of course!" And with that she went into action. "Husband, get the stove lit and bring in some fresh cream and butter from the cool house." The food I had imagined began appearing on the table, and soon we were eating the best food anyone could want.

His face the color of ashes, the truck driver tied in the chair shook with fear. About three centimeters from his quivering face, the bullet-headed Commandant spoke with an intense whisper that occasionally spattered spit on the white face. "How … I want to know … how a feeble old man with two children stole your truck full of tools. I want to know why you did not report this immediately to the Gestapo. I want to know why you are telling me that your truck broke down, but we find this limping old coot driving it across the countryside! I want to know why I shouldn't send you to the firing squad. You sound so righteous! Tell me, what do you have to say to that?" The truck driver had no hope.

Escape Five

"EARLY IS BETTER THAN LATE"

The Journal of Henry Gutmann
A farm by the side of the road, Germany - September 1939

I felt wonderful, warmed by the stove, full of delicious farm food, bathed in hot water, and tucked into a downy bed. This sweet couple, we learned, were working with the Resistance, trying to hinder Hitler's cruel practices. Sharing our adventures of trying to escape from the Nazis, we all laughed as Opa described the clumsy Gestapo and our various disguises. With giant yawns interrupting our tales, our hosts had taken us upstairs to a comfortable guest room where we barely could get out of our clothes before we fell into a deep sleep.

Nothing seems to go by more quickly than a good night's sleep. With a gentle shake, Opa began waking us up. Standing there winding his gold watch, which he did every morning, he said cheerfully, "Come, boys, I know it's early, but it is better than late. We must be up and away."

Hans, as usual, made it much harder to wake him up. Pulling his pillow over his head, his muffled voice said, "Leave me alone. I don't want to get up."

It was funny to hear Opa say to him, *"So how long will you lie there, slacker?"*

Somehow, the memory of seeing a gun pointed at him roused him and soon we followed Opa downstairs. Our hostess had already made coffee and spooned hot oatmeal in bowls with brown sugar and clotted cream. I didn't think that I would be able to ever eat another bite after last night's meal, but my hunger came rushing back and we all managed to clean our bowls and munch down a handful of homemade biscuits. After the dishes were cleared off the table, Opa filled the tank with gas from our hosts' supply, paid them well, and left instructions for the man and his wife to get in touch with men from the

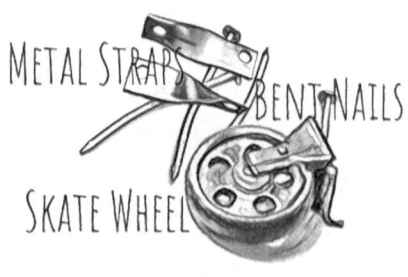

METAL STRAPS
BENT NAILS
SKATE WHEEL

underground. They would know how to take care of Mr. Eyebrow, who was still tied up, looking like a human sausage. With a gracious goodbye to our wonderful hosts, we climbed into the truck and headed back onto the road. Our next adventure was a real doozy! You will not believe how Grandfather got us out of it and the incredible device he made from an antique roller skate wheel, two metal strips, four bent nails, and a lot of inertia.

However, we had a significant detour first. What started out as a lovely day, with the sun shining and birds flying overhead, began going badly right as we arrived at the fork in the road leading to Munster. Even though we were only traveling at forty kph (that means kilometers per hour), with no problems we would arrive in Osnabrück at around four o'clock.

We didn't make it by four. Actually, we didn't make it at all.

Standing at the intersection was an attractive woman waving a red scarf. I knew my grandfather would not pass her by. He slowed and rolled down the truck window as she walked up to speak to him.

"Oh please, sir, I was pushed out of a car this morning by some bad men and I have no way of reaching my home in Munster. It is too far to walk." Standing there with disheveled hair, in a very tight dress, holding a pair of red shoes in one hand and her scarf in the other, she tilted her head to one side. "Please, please sir, you look like a very kind person." Her voice a bit oily and the way she blinked her eyes made me nervous.

"I am so sorry for your situation, miss," Opa answered. "We are actually headed for Osnabrück, not Munster. Could we take you in that direction? I am sure you could get transportation back to Munster."

"Oh no, sir. I must get to Munster. Could you please, please just take me as far as the city outskirts where I could get transport. I have no money but I would appreciate it so much." At that, she stepped onto the truck running board, reached in the window, and caressed Grandfather's shoulder. He was uncomfortable and I could tell.

He pointed toward a weathered sign along the road to Munster.

"I know of an eatery and inn just 2 kilometers up the road, but then we must turn back. We will——" Before he could say anything else, she reached in, kissed him on the cheek, hopped down, and ran around to the door on our side. Pulling the door open, she squeezed in beside me, pushing Hans closer to Opa.

"My, what handsome looking young men you have here, father." With a fake smile and much wiggling, she patted each of us on the knee. Opa, with an uncharacteristic frown on his face, put the truck into gear and pulled onto the road to Munster.

We had driven not more than a kilometer when, rounding a curve, we saw the black-and-red-striped pole of a Gestapo checkpoint. Five or six heavily armed soldiers stood guard. Grandfather slowed down, but it was too late to stop and turn around. They had already seen us and no way could this truck outrun the military vehicles parked by the road.

My heart leapt into my throat. We slowed to a stop at the guard building. Smiling as if he were greeting an old friend, Grandfather rolled down his window, saluting the soldier.

"Good afternoon, Sergeant, we were—"

"Silence," the soldier yelled. "Get out of the truck! We know who you are. You have stolen a vehicle and these two boys with you are imposters. They are not Hitler Youth. All of you are going to the prison camps. Now!" He looked over, noticing the woman sitting next to me. "Well, hello beautiful." He then whistled and shouted to his fellow soldiers. "Look who came back to see us, boys." Turning to look, I noticed that under her heavy makeup and rouged lips she had gone pale. But, holding her head up, she stepped out of the truck, looked coyly over at the guard and whined, "Well, at least I brought what you were looking for, officer."

It was amazing to watch my grandfather smile at the red-faced soldier, turn to us, and gently say, "Come, boys, I think this gentleman wants us to climb out of the truck." He stepped down, helped us climb from the cab, and followed the soldier meekly.

Clicking behind us in high-heeled shoes, the woman followed until one of the other soldiers yelled. "Hey you, floozie! You are staying here. It will be way more fun than where they are going." She shrugged and pushed her chin out, giving the soldier a defiant look.

"And Heil Hitler to you, Nazi patsy," she said with poisoned lips, then spit on the ground. Somehow, I felt worse for her than for us.

The railroad tracks were right beside the checkpoint. Three wooden cattle cars were lined up on the siding beside the main tracks. Before we could say or do anything, we were shoved into the front cattle car, the heavy wooden door slammed behind us and chains padlocked us in. Through the openings in the wide wooden slats, we heard the sergeant give an order to the soldiers. "See that you flag down the evening train and make sure these three railroad cars are picked up and taken to the camps."

With a rueful sigh, Opa said, "A valuable lesson for you boys to learn, *'the lips of a loose woman drip honey and her speech is smoother than oil but in the end she is bitter as wormwood, like a sharp cut from a double-edged sword. Her feet go down to death; her steps lead straight to the grave.'"*

"Opa, was she a bad woman?" asked Hans, shrugging his shoulders.

"We don't know, boys. We never judge a book by its cover, as you know." He hinted about our secret-compartment books which had been left behind on the truck. "We do know that, in the same way as there are evil men, there can be unstable women who give no thought to their ways, who can lead you astray. We are told, *'Stay far away from her, do not go near the door of her house. For your integrity will be stolen by others and your dignity to one who is cruel.'"* His words made me shiver.

I looked around the inside of the railroad car. A pretty standard boxcar with no exit except the locked sliding door. Made with heavy wooden boards, it would have taken hours or days to saw through, even if we had a standard size saw. Opa's Swiss Army Knife would never do it. No way to escape this time. The inside was empty, except for a stack of huge railroad ties in one corner. They were at least twenty centimeters square and more than two meters long. Much too heavy for even all three of us to move.

Quiet descended on us and a feeling of helplessness as well. Opa looked unperturbed, but I think he might have been putting on a good face so my brother and I would not be too frightened. As hours slipped by, he paced slowly from one side of the car to the other. Suddenly, we all heard a soft rustling sound. A mouse? A snake? The sound came from behind the pile of railroad ties. With total confidence, Opa walked over to the stack, reached behind it, and pulled up … a … girl?! Yes, a young, very thin, blonde girl just about my age. Her blue eyes were huge and she looked terrified.

"Well, look what what we have here," said Opa softly. He looked into her face, but didn't have to bend over much because her eyes almost met his. As tall as me, I think. "My, my. What is your name, sweetheart?"

She looked at Grandfather with her big blue eyes. Her face tightened and she answered bravely, "My name is Hannah."

"So tell us about yourself, Hannah," he said kindly. She went on to tell us about being born and growing up in a small town called Senden where many Jewish families had settled. When the Nazi government began rounding up Jews, they herded almost everyone in town, including her whole family, to the railroad tracks, loading them all into cattle cars headed for what she called the "death camps." They had arrived early at the train, so her father had the extra time to hide her behind the railroad ties. She said it was lucky she had not been seen as they unloaded the train at the camps. As she spoke of her parents, head bowed, lips quivering, tears splashed onto her skirt.

"Don't be worried, Hannah. There was no luck involved, child." Opa said as he shook his head. *"Good people will be rescued from trouble."* He rummaged around in his massive coat and pulled out a tin containing two biscuits and some jam and cheese spread. "Here, young lady. I know you must be hungry. The boys had a hearty dinner last night and breakfast this morning. They are very willing to let you have this small portion." I wasn't so sure about that, but I looked over at Hans.

He smiled, glad to share. My stomach felt the pinch already. Breakfast seemed days ago, but Hannah looked like she hadn't eaten in months.

"Well, Hannah, here we are and we shall be known as the Four 'H' Club. Hannah, Henry, Hans, and Humpty Dumpty." We laughed. We all shook hands and introduced ourselves. Opa introduced himself as Humpty. A faint smile crossed Hannah's face, a good sign.

"Now we need to figure out how we can get out of here." Grandfather walked around the car looking carefully at everything. I could tell he was thinking hard because he had begun whistling. He ended his walk by the pile of railroad ties. Bending over, he tried to move one but only managed to scoot it about ten millimeters. "This will work wonderfully! It will make a perfect battering ram."

Hannah looked over at me and, with disbelief in her voice, asked, "Does your grandfather think we can really escape? We can barely move one of those ties, much less pick it up and use it as a battering ram."

"If he believes it, he can achieve it," said Hans hopefully. I shrugged my shoulders. Each adventure had seemed more impossible than the one before. Each escape was more amazing, which made me willing to try again.

"Heave ho, all together now. We want to move the biggest railroad tie until it is parallel with the side of the car." So together we pushed and shoved a few millimeters at a time until it lined up facing the direction Opa pointed.

"Now Hannah, you sit down and have something to eat while we work on our battering ram. Here, Henry, take my Swiss Army Knife with the can opener blade. Do you see this crack right in the middle here? I want you to carve away on it until it is wide enough to put your thumb into it." He began pulling things out of his pockets.

Hannah sat on another of the ties with her knees together, eating her biscuit like a little bird, one crumb at a time. Hans looked at the biscuit with a hungry longing, so she offered him half, but under no circumstances would he take anything from her. He had to show that he was strong. I guess I did too, so I focused on carving away at the crack in the railroad tie. We had something to prove now.

A row of items had been placed on one end of the wood. It sure didn't look as if anyone could make a battering ram with a metal roller skate wheel, a large bolt, two metal strips, and a few bent nails.

Hannah finished her biscuit, wiped her mouth, stared first at the strange items, then at Grandfather. I could tell she didn't think that this would work. He took the wheel and slipped it into the slot that I had widened. It fit loosely.

"Henry, use your can opener blade to carve two grooves on either side of the wheel, here and here." When I finished, the bolt got pushed through the hole in the wheel and fit perfectly into the grooves. Using the back end of his Swiss Army Knife, Grandfather straightened the bent nails, took the two strips of metal, and hammered them into the wood to hold the bolt in place.

"Aha! Perfect! *'If you don't know, learn how; if you are stupid, gain some common sense.'*"

"We now have a one-wheeled scooter. Two wheels would work better, but one is all we have. The weight of the log and the motion of the train will create inertia. Force in motion. Very powerful force. Now let us turn it over." Doing that proved harder than it seemed, but with the use of Grandfather's Swiss Army Knife, his folding cane, a broken piece of the wood I had chiseled out, and all four of us lifting, we finally flipped it over. It wobbled a bit, but we could actually feel it roll when we pushed it.

At that moment the train car jolted and started moving forward. We all held on to our wooden battering ram so it would not roll to the front of the car. Hannah, small and thin, still showed us her strength. Together we held it in place as Opa explained the strategy. "It is good we worked on this early before the train started. Once we started moving it would have been much harder to position our battering ram. Now, do you see that spot at the front corner of the car where the wood is splintered a bit? We are going to point our beam right for that corner. If I remember right, this railroad track starts a downhill slope in about twenty kilometers and has a sharp curve at the bottom. This train will have to slow down to keep from going off the track. At that point we will set our beam going, give it a mighty push and kinetic motion will do the work. Bam! It will punch a hole in the wall."

Once again, he was right. The train gradually sped up and after a while started going downhill. Our heavy, one-wheeled scooter tried to start rolling toward the front of the car.

"Not yet, team! Not yet!" Grandfather cautioned as we all held onto the giant rolling railroad tie. "Wait … wait …" We heard the squeal of brakes. "Not yet, team." The metallic clang of one railroad car thumped loudly into the next as the train braked for the curve. We heard our car clang into the one in front of us. "Now!" yelled Grandfather. With a mighty push, we let go.

Very slowly the railroad tie began to move. With Opa steering at the back, all of us pushing, and the train slowing down, it began to pick up speed. Faster and faster, it rolled toward the front corner. It wobbled as Opa steered it for a few more seconds and then … he let it go. It seemed like it happened in slow motion. We all held our breaths. CRASH! Wood splintered, metal twisted, bolts ripped from their holes. As the dust cleared, we knew it had worked. Our battering ram, sticking halfway out of the front of the railroad car, had punched a gaping hole a dozen people could climb through. We all cheered.

Hans shouted, "Let it roll and punch a hole!" We were far enough back in the line that train guards wouldn't have heard the crash. Hannah, gaping at Grandfather, had a look of amazement on her face.

"This is only one small victory. As you can see from the tracks rushing past," Opa said as he pointed at the ground outside the hole, "the train is still moving too fast to jump off."

He said, "Ha, now we wait until dark when the train reaches the bottom of the hill. I will unhook our car, we'll roll to a stop, then we'll hop out." He waved his hand like a magician. I think he was showing off a bit for Hannah, yet perhaps now she started to believe my grandfather could do all that and more. It was getting close to sunset. We didn't have long to wait.

"Here, let us celebrate," announced Opa, pulling more food from his pockets and handing it to us. Some fruit. Biscuits. And more jam. With another flourish, he began unwinding a plastic tube from around his waist. "And water." The tube was folded over and pinched on one end. It had a cork in the other. He took the empty metal tin that he had given to Hannah and poured clear water into it from the tube. Amazing how much water he kept pouring out until all of us had had something to drink. Even Opa.

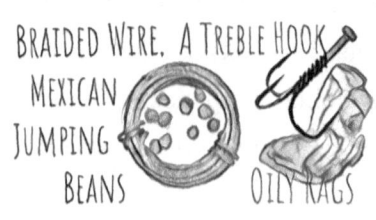

BRAIDED WIRE. A TREBLE HOOK
MEXICAN JUMPING BEANS
OILY RAGS

"'*Drink water from your own cistern, find running water in your own well,*' it tells us in the Good Book. Does it not, boys?" We, of course, knew what he quoted from, but Hannah looked puzzled. I think at some point we would have to tell her more about our mysterious Grandfather. There would be time for that after our next adventure, which involved twelve jumping beans, a treble hook, a spool of braided wire, some oily rags, and a large sheet of metal.

"In the meantime," said Opa, "we can all take a nap."

Anger, frustration, and fear kept the Commandant from sleep. Trapped on a narrow cot in a back room where he had to remain on duty, he too found himself imprisoned by his assignment as the head of the Gestapo in Munster. Others might sleep. He could not. The head of the Munster Gestapo force struggled from his sleepless cot and slumped down over his desk to write a telegram for the head of the prison camp at Dachau. The Commandant, now convinced the old man was a spy, felt compelled to catch him. Way too clever. This man could look old and feeble yet overpower a Nazi mayor, pull a heavily loaded truck out of the mud, and convince the police that the boys were Nazi youth. There was no time to waste. The man and the two boys must be brought into custody to find out what they knew.

Escape Six

"LIBERTY IS BETTER THAN BONDAGE"

The Journal of Henry Gutmann
On the train to a prison camp, Germany - September 1939

The track did, in fact, level out and the train seemed to be picking up speed. I had no idea how we were going to get off. When we had been loaded into the cattle car, we had seen at least six or seven cars ahead of us full of people being transported to the prison camps. In the fading light, I turned to Opa and, over the the noise of the giant metal wheels, asked, "Are all those people heading to the camps going to die?"

With an uncharacteristic sorrow that seldom crossed his face, Opa nodded his head. "Yes, I believe so, and God hates it. *'There are six things the Lord hates, actually seven that are detestable to Him: proud eyes, a lying tongue, hands that shed innocent blood, a heart that makes wicked plans, feet that are quick to rush into evil, a false witness who twists the truth, and a leader who creates conflict in his own country.'* Hitler is doing all those things. But don't forget, my friends, God is still good. He has more power than a thousand armies and is in control of everything." With that, even in the gathering darkness I could imagine the twinkle in his eye. Hans had dozed off immediately and was still sleeping like a corpse.

"What are we going to do now?" asked Hannah in her timid voice.

From the darkness, Opa's voice was clear. "Well, first we must roust out the sleeping one here."

He ruffled his hair, but Hans merely groaned, "Let me sleep," and turned over.

"I have to repeat the same bit of wisdom, *'When are you going to get up from your sleep? You tell us to let you sleep. You say, just let me snooze a little longer, I need to fold my hands to rest. But then poverty like a robber will take everything from you and all your wealth will be stolen by an armed soldier.'"*

Hans finally began to rub his eyes in the gloom.

Hannah said, "I will be amazed if we actually escape from this train."

"Opa can do it, he is our man," mumbled Hans. "If he can't do it, no one can." I had to snort and shake my head.

"What can we do now, Opa?" We watched in fear and trepidation as Grandfather took off his oversize coat and began to crawl through the hole we had made with our battering ram. He looked so trim and slender without his coat. I wanted to try it on to see how much it weighed. As quick as a ferret, Opa slipped down to the coupling that held us to the rest of the train. We had been the last car they hooked up, so we were at the end of the line. When the train began to slow down, he pulled on the lever that opened the hook. With a metallic clang, the coupling released and we were on our own. Slowly the train pulled away into the darkness and we eventually drifted to a stop.

"Quick, boys … er, girl and boys … uh, team, hand me my coat and let's get off this evil train."

Hans could barely lift it, so I had to help, passing the heavy woolen coat down through the hole. Opa's battering ram had been amazingly effective. We followed and, with Opa in the lead, we scrambled down the gravel slope and into the tall grass at the side of the track.

We were free! Off in the distance, the fading lights of the "death train" moved into the night. To the left, a dark forest of huge spruce trees loomed. I recognized them because we had always chopped one down for Christmas, but these were twenty times bigger. No problem, though. Grandfather's bright flashlight led the way.

After an hour of walking in almost total darkness, we came into a clearing where a creek wound its way through the woods. A bright, almost full moon gave us more than enough light.

"Here," announced our fearless leader, "we will spend the night. Henry, you and Hannah collect some twigs and branches for a fire. If you break them off from right at the base of the tree, they will be the driest and easiest to light. Hans, you take these tins and fill them with water, and I will light a fire." Something we had not seen before came out of Opa's pockets. A piece of stone and a curved metal grip about the size of a bracelet. Strips of paper from my notebook were piled on top of the twigs and dried leaves we collected. He began striking the stone with the metal rod and sparks flew into the twigs and paper. After about three tries, the paper lit and, surprise, a spark caught and became a flame igniting the paper and wood, which soon turned into a nice size fire.

As we warmed our hands, Opa explained, "Flint is a very hard stone that you can find almost anywhere near a rock outcropping. When struck with a piece of steel, sparks fly off and light a fire. Matches get wet, lighters run out of fuel, but flint and steel always works. I am sorry, all I have for dinner is some dried beef." We sat by the fire, chewed on our beef jerky, and drank cool water from the creek. Although we were tired, Opa gently coaxed Hannah to tell us her story.

Her family was Jewish. They had immigrated to Germany from Russia during the persecution of Jews in that country.

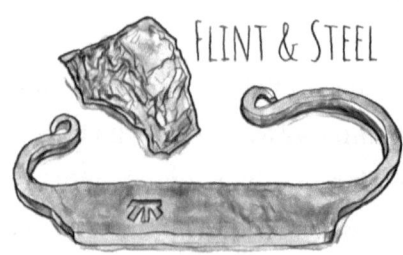

They thought they would be secure in Munster. It was not to be. Within only a few years the attitudes had changed and now the Jews were again having to flee for their lives. She, her father, her mother, and one sister had been rounded up, kept in a ghetto for weeks with hardly any food, then finally shoved on a train to the camps.

"As the youngest in my family, father always tried to protect me. He created the space behind the railroad ties, covered me with a piece of sacking, and whispered in my ear, 'God has a plan for you. He will spare your life.' Father told me not to move or make any noise. Being obedient to my father was always important to me. I really don't know how they did not discover me hiding behind those wooden beams when they unloaded my family at the camps, but they didn't. I rode the empty car all the way back to Munster and waited another whole day until the door opened and you climbed on. It was a miracle. My father was right."

"You are wise to listen to your father, Hannah. We are all told to *'keep your father's command and don't forsake your mother's teaching. Tie them always to your heart, fasten them around your neck. When you walk, they will guide you; when you sleep they will watch over you; when you wake up they will speak to you.'"*

"But I don't understand how these people can do such mean things and get away with it," whimpered Hannah, bowing her head onto her knees.

Opa put a hand on her shoulder to reassure her. "They will not get away with these cruel acts, Hannah, *'for those who plot evil with a devious heart and stir up conflict will have disaster overtake them in an instant and be destroyed without anyone to help.'* Now, team, we must get some rest."

Opa crawled under the fragrant spruce trees where the branches hung down to the ground and showed us an open space at the base of the tree, like a ready-made tent. We piled up pine needles and, even if they were a bit prickly, they were soft and fragrant. We curled up like woodland creatures and fell into a deep sleep.

The smell of something cooking woke me. Squinting in broad daylight, I crawled out of our spruce tent. Opa had kindled a fire and was cooking fish.

"Good morning, Henry. I dug some fat worms from the dirt. I had hooks with fishing line and these hungry trout almost jumped out of the stream to get caught. These willow branches are working well as a grill. A bit of salt and some wild herbs growing along the riverbank have provided a real feast." The peeled branches held the fish in place over the fire and four giant trout were roasting away, giving off a wonderful smell. My mouth was already watering.

After filling our stomachs with delicious grilled trout, we washed up in the creek, cleared away any traces of our camp, used Grandfather's magnetic needle to determine our direction, and headed off through the woods, hoping to find a friendly family that could help us get to Holland.

After about three hours of walking, we heard the sound of someone chopping wood. A clearing ahead revealed a strange sight. Three shacks were surrounded by dozens of weird sculptures on tall poles, and a grizzled man with an oversize head was swinging a large double-bladed ax, making kindling. The sculptures looked like stars, moons, planets, and solar bodies. They were all superstitious symbols made from strings, bones, bits of glass, and metal, and were shaped to look like angry faces with eyes that seemed to be watching us even when we moved. We approached the wrinkle-faced man.

"Greetings, sir," hailed our ever-cheerful grandfather. "I and my grandchildren have gotten lost in the woods and would most assuredly appreciate some help if you are able to give it."

"The voices told me you would come," rasped a gravelly voice as if from lungs filled with broken pieces, like the rattling of glass, metal, and bones hanging from the strange sculptures around us. He stood staring at us from strange bulbous eyes. The only motion was the bobbing of his oversize head. He stared until I started getting nervous. A breeze whisked through the trees, quivering his creations that mimicked his voice. "You will stay. Stay for a long time." The voice rattled in his chest. "I have a place for you and the boys, and a place for the girl." A menacing grimace crossed his face.

This guy creeped me out. Hannah moved close to me and grabbed my arm. Even Hans tried to grab the back of my shirt, pulling me back and away from this leathery man.

As usual, Opa did not seem to be fazed a bit. "Thank you for your kind offer. I am Mr. Humperdinck and these are my grandchildren, Henry, Hans, and Hannah. We are needing directions and some transportation to the town of Osnabrück. We are not too far, are we? I would be glad to pay you for your trouble."

I, for sure, did not want to ride anywhere with this strange character. Hans and Hannah looked at each other, then over at me. We all had apprehensive looks on our faces. Opa did not seem to be bothered at all, but he never was.

"Do you have any sort of vehicle in which you could transport us to the nearest town?" Without even answering the question, the guy shouldered his ax, turned, and motioned for us to follow. He walked, hunched over with a decided limp, to the smallest of the three buildings. All of them, even the main house, were made of sheet metal, welded to iron poles, bent into bizarre shapes. It resembled a giant birdcage twisted by some mighty hand. The door opened. With the unexpected speed of a snake, he slithered around behind us and raised his ax to strike. He backed us into the cage and swung the door shut with a vicious clang! "Yes," he cackled, "you will stay with me for a long time. Especially the girl." Another chain, another lock sealed us in. I was getting tired of chains and locks. The pop-eyed man gave us a final grin and walked into the largest building.

"Oh no," wailed Hannah. "Now we will never get out. We are going to die in here."

"Shh," whispered Opa. "Don't worry, we will find a way out, I assure you. Come, come now. All will be fine." But it did not seem to be fine. The cage we were in had nothing but a concrete floor, a pile of garbage, rusty iron, and some leftover sheets of metal. "Here, Henry, you comfort Hannah. Hans, I need you to make an inventory of what is lying around here, and I need some time to think." Humming a tune, he then said, "We do need to get out of here. *'When you are in someone's trap, go to them and in a nice way ask him to release you. If they won't then don't rest until you have been released. Get out like a gazelle escaping from a trap, like a bird flying from a net.'*"

I had never comforted a hysterical girl before, but I did the best I could by explaining that our grandfather had gotten us out of many tight spots before. "He is like a genius, I promise. This is no trouble for him. Trust him. He has more brain power in his earlobe than that crazy giant out there has in his entire oversize head. The last time Opa got us out of a mess it was much worse than this." I began telling Hannah some of the stories of our adventures.

The sound of chopping had resumed outside in the sun, but we sat down on the ground in the gloom. Pinpricks of sunlight lanced through tiny holes in the metal roof. It started to get hot in our birdcage. Hans counted and stacked pieces of junk iron and Opa retreated to one lopsided corner, deep in thought. After a while, I noticed he was reading from a slender book he pulled from one of his many pockets.

"Well, Hans, what do we have in our inventory?"

"Opa, we are sunk. All I can find is rusty junk," he mumbled morosely. "It's mostly metal, a pile of shiny aluminum squares, some braided wire, a roll of twine, a can with the bottom rusted out, and one that has motor oil in it. There is a tub of miscellaneous rusty nails, screws, eye hooks, and washers."

"That's good. That's very good, very good," answered Opa.

Finally, darkness started to blanket us in our wire cage. The weird guy stopped chopping and went inside. The temperature in our oven went down, but the metal sheets still radiated heat. They clinked and ticked as they cooled. My voice, tired from the stories, went silent. Quiet settled around us. With a burst of energy, Opa leapt to his feet, clanged his head on the tin roof, then laughed. We all laughed with him.

"Now, my young orchestra, we will make light and music!" declared Grandfather.

"First, Hans, tear those oily rags into strips which will make oil lamps so we are able to see." I wondered what he had in mind. With typical Opa efficiency, he picked up a handful of the metal squares and, with his Swiss Army Knife, bent them into bowls with a pinched crimp at one end. On the other end, he bent up a vertical flap and threaded the strips through the pinched part. After pouring a bit of the oil into the bowl, he got Hans to light the wicks on fire with the flint and steel. The result amazed me. The wicks burned brightly, soaking up the oil. The flame was reflected in the shiny aluminum and with only three lamps it was bright enough to see everything in our "cage."

"See, boys and girl, *'God's righteousness is his lamp that shines inside us.'* As The Book says, *'The ways of right-living people glow like a sunrise; the longer they live, the brighter they shine.'"* The warm glow of the hand-made lamps cheered us up quite a bit. "These are like the lamps made in Bible times, only they used clay hardened in the fire. Ours are metal and work even better because of the shiny reflector. It actually doubles the amount of light because the flame is seen twice. Now," he said as he rubbed his hands together, "we will try to find a way out of this chicken coop."

"Hans, your job is the hardest." He handed him the spool of twine. "Tie this large washer on one end of the twine. If you will look carefully, there is a metal handle on the closest window of the main house. Toss the washer through the handle. It will take you a while, but keep trying. In the meantime, Henry, you must take three of the nails and create treble hooks like this. Hannah, you must begin untangling this pile of braided wire and coil it neatly in the box."

Hans managed to push his arm through a hole in the metal cage and began swinging the string in a circle and letting it go at the right time so it arced toward the house. More than three or four meters away, at first he could not even get close. As he practiced, he kept getting closer and closer. I took a short piece of wire and wrapped it around the heads of the bent nails, creating what looked like a large, three-pronged fishing hook.

I soon had a large treble hook and Hannah had wound the wire neatly in the box. Hans kept trying. "My arm is getting tired," he said. "Henry, I think it is your turn." I tried to get my arm through the hole, but could not squeeze it through.

"Let me try," said Hannah softly. "We played a game of ring toss my parents had on our back porch. We had a large ring tied to the ceiling. You stood across the porch and swung the ring, trying to get it to hook on a nail at the other end of the porch. I was sort of the family champion." Without any trouble, she slipped her arm through the hole and began swinging the washer. I watched, amazed, as the washer, shining in the lamplight, arced across the distance to the house and on the first try, dropped right through the open handle!

"Wow," I said under my breath. "That was amazing, Hannah!" She smiled humbly and I think a blush rose into her face.

"Hannah, that was a wonderful bit of skill you showed us. You have proved very valuable to our team. I think we must keep you around," I said. She looked very pleased with herself, and the light of the small oil lamps lit up her blonde hair like spun gold. Her blushing cheeks made her look a bit … angelic.

The treble hook tied to the wire was then hooked through the washer and pulled until it hooked on the metal window.

"Now, we must tune the instrument." Picking up a slender rod, Opa waved his baton like the conductor of a symphony orchestra. It made us all laugh. With his grey hair sticking out in every direction, he looked like one. He began twisting the wire with his baton. It looked like the tuning peg on my father's violin. As he twisted, we could hear the wire "pinging" with a higher pitch at each turn. Plucking the wire softly, the note reverberated across the distance to the house and caused the metal door to hum with the same note.

From his pocket, Opa pulled out a wooden matchbox, but what fell out of the box when he opened it were about twelve round nuts. "Look what I have, boys. They call these Mexican jumping beans. They actually don't jump, but each one has a tiny worm in it that wiggles around when the bean is heated." He spilled them all onto the sheet metal and started heating the underside with a lamp.

To my wondering eyes, the beans began to hop and wiggle. The effect electrified us. Each hop made a "clink" on the sheet metal amplified like a violin, transmitted through the wire to the metal frame of the house. It was the eeriest sound I had ever heard. Grandfather added to the clinking of the beans by running a rusty piece of metal along the wire. A hair-curling, skin-tingling moan echoed around the compound. "I think this will amplify Mr. Superstitious' fears significantly." He did it again, only louder. Each turn on the baton and the pitch went up to an ear-piercing shriek. It was so loud and terrifying I had to put my hands over my ears. One more time he scraped, starting with a slow quaver and climbing to a sound that seemed to vibrate inside my head. Twice more he played his fiddle, each time louder and more intense than before.

Suddenly the back door flew open and, wearing only some type of nightgown, the man with the strange head came running into the yard. Just as he did, Grandfather placed the rusted out can against the sheet metal sounding board and spoke. His voice, pitched an octave or two higher than normal, sounded like a demented alien and reverberated around the yard.

"Listen, old man ... You don't know what you have done! You must release your prisoners and give them everything they ask for, or the wrath of all the spirits will descend on you and melt your skin from your body! Do it! Do it NOW!" He added a wild screech with his metal violin-pick.

Leaping, with his eyes bugging almost out of his oversize head, the weird man ran inside the house. Within moments, he emerged carrying a handful of keys and began fumbling with the lock on our cage. He shook so badly, it took him three tries to unlock and pull the door open. We gratefully eased through the open door while backing away from him. In his terrified state, he fell to his knees and offered a set of keys to us.

"Take the car, here, take the car. It is around front. Here is a bag of food and water. Go. Just go." His voice shook with fear. Opa stepped over and, with all the calm of one borrowing the car keys from a friend, he took them and the bag of food, then looked into the eyes of the demented man. He spoke to him in a serious but kind voice.

"Friend, you must change your ways. If you do, I will pour out my wisdom to you, I will make you understand my teachings. But if you refuse to listen when I call and pay no attention when I reach out ... Then you

will call to me but I will not answer; You will look for me but will not find me."

Lightheartedly, he then said, "Do not fear about your car. We will send the keys and a notice of where we leave the vehicle back to you when we are done with it." Quickly, with purpose, he turned and walked around the building. What we found was a surprise to all of us.

There sat a vintage, but well-cared-for, 12-cylinder Daimler.

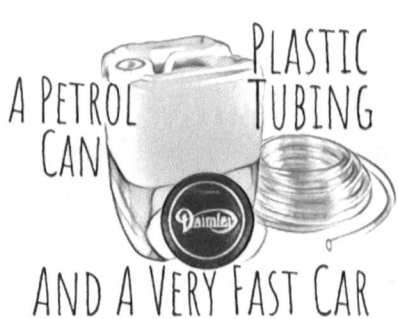

A PETROL CAN, PLASTIC TUBING AND A VERY FAST CAR

Very unusual to see this well-built piece of German engineering sitting in front of the strange metal house. As the sun came peeking over the trees, all four of us piled into the sleek Daimler, which started with a quiet purr and then built up to a mighty growl, and drove away with our backs to the light of the rising sun.

No comment necessary, but Hans still had to celebrate our departure with an ode to our grandfather's phenomenal musical instrument. "The weird guy trapped us, you see, but Opa's violin set us free, whoopee!"

I held my head, but Hannah said, "I think that's cute."

"Please don't encourage him." My comment was drowned out by the wind and the roar of the Daimler.

Our next escape was simple. A very fast car, a clear tube, and three cans of petrol.

The light of day never shone in the Commandant's office. The flickering fluorescent bulbs in the ceiling cast deeper shadows on the narrow face of the Gestapo leader. Pale blue eyes shone intently even in the gloom. The entire Gestapo force, it seemed, was crammed into the dark space around his metal desk. Multiple dents in the desktop and sides were signs of his wrath. Today was different. The anger was bottled, under pressure evidenced only by the veins standing out on his temples, string tight neck sinews, and working jaw muscles as he spoke. "They have escaped again. The rail car they were in had a hole punched in the front wall. It is obvious now they are three spies disguised as an old man with two young boys. We have code-named his group "The Trinity." Five thousand marks to the man that catches them. And they must be taken alive."

#

"Safety is better than Danger"

The Journal of Henry Gutmann
Back on the road to Osnabrück, Germany - September 1939

Hans, mimicking the wrinkled old guy, had us laughing so hard I got the hiccups. Mostly it was a huge relief to be away from that creepy place. Hannah giggled, too, but soon we all drifted into silence. We had eaten brown bread, smoked mackerel, and fruit washed down with a jug of water. We felt comfortably full. Not the delicious breakfast we had enjoyed at the farmhouse, but tasty and nutritious; we were glad for it.

"Opa, how did you know that man would let us out?" Hannah asked. She called him Opa for the first time and I could see he was pleased. Still, I marveled to see how some rusty nails, a handful of Mexican jumping beans, and some braided wire could have created that kind of effect. But, to tell the truth, I too would have run from the house without any clothes on after hearing that noise.

"A deep truth applies to all people everywhere, my sweet fraülein. When anyone disregards the teachings of our Creator, they are immediately put in the position of having to explain many things which cannot be explained with logic or science, a place where darkness rules. Without the light, many people turn to their own twisted spiritism. A belief that good or evil spirits make things happen we don't understand. Our captor had been caught up in his fear or worship of these beings. It was an easy task to tap into his fears. Doing it at night helped." He smiled at Hannah and her eyes reflected the same kind of growing respect that both Hans and I had developed over the years.

"What I want to know, Opa," said Hans, "is how did you get that horrible noise out of that wire contraption?"

"Not complicated," he chuckled. "Do you remember when I showed you how to make a telephone out of two tin cans and a string? Well, the principle is the same with any stringed instrument, any speaker or amplification device. That house was made entirely of sheet metal. The wire strung from our cage was the origination of the vibrations that were amplified down the wire to the house. The house became the sounding box. Hans, you tortured us when you began learning how to play the cello. I am sure you remember the horrible screeches you made when you played a sour note." I laughed, holding my ears as I remembered the sound. "Same principle," he continued, "only this time we were doing that on a giant scale. It sure worked pretty well, didn't it?"

Since Opa was being talkative, I decided to ask him about something that had been rolling around in my head for a couple of days. It was the memory of the woman in the red dress. On one level, she had seemed sly and conniving. On another, she came across as proud and arrogant. I didn't know what to think. Knowing that Opa would have more to say, I asked him.

"Opa, why did you warn us about that woman we picked up at the fork to Munster? She made me nervous, but then I felt sad for her."

For a long time, he remained silent, until I thought he was either ignoring me or hadn't heard.

"You are right to have compassion, Henry. We don't know what abuses and difficulties she has lived with, but every human has a choice. People who have been hurt can choose to forgive those who have abused them and find freedom, or they can drag around chains of bitterness for the rest of their lives."

"What happens when they don't forgive, Opa?" asked Hannah.

"Bitterness can easily make them angry and defiant. They will make bad choices and persuade others to go along in their foolishness. Be careful of them. *'With persuasive words they can lead you astray. They will seduce you with smooth talk. Those that follow will be like an ox going to be killed, like a deer stepping into a trap.'*"

Wow, that gave me some serious thoughts to chew on. I could tell by their silence that Hans and Hannah were thinking it over too.

Whizzing down the smooth road in the classic sports car was a luxury we had not expected. We were a bit tight, packed into a two-seater, but the precision of German engineering made it comfortable. The 12-cylinder engine hummed under the hood like the Vienna Boys' Choir. What a grand way to travel! Plus, it was a huge relief to be heading in the right direction, away from our captors. With the two windows down and the wind whipping our hair, it felt very free indeed. I knew there was another adventure ahead, but at the time I did not know it would involve—if you can believe it—tape, scissors, foam rubber, and a kind of lizard called a gecko.

"Here, Henry, look in the glove box and see if you can find another map. My trusty almanac accidentally got left in the tool truck." When I opened the leather-covered door to the compartment, a pile of papers, booklets, and pamphlets fell out, all with strange symbols printed on them. It looked like propaganda for the weird beliefs the old guy had been living under. Somewhere in the pile, I did find a map of Germany. Old, yellowed, and cracked, it had been in use long before they made the car. Once unfolded, it presented all the major cities and roads, with various other points of interest.

I saw our hometown of Munster. We were trying to get away from that. Up north was Bremen, farther even, Hamburg, and almost 100 kilometers beyond that, Denmark. It seemed too far to go. Holland was closer.

"To the north," pointed Opa, "the town of Osnabrück near the Ems river, where Vilka's parents live. A straight shot to Holland from there."

"Opa, we need to look for signs to Osnabrück. That will take us toward Holland and it's only about 40 kilometers from here."

"What we need to find before that, my three H's, is some petrol. This car has become one of the best machines Germany ever produced, but it runs on petrol and we will have to fill it up soon."

Off in the distance, a giant tanker truck appeared alongside the road. We were cautious as we pulled up to it, but the flat tire made it evident someone had probably abandoned it.

"Opa, this was like a miracle! You ask for gas and presto, there is more gas than we could ever use." In a jiffy, Hans and I leapt out of the car and climbed on top of the tank on the truck. Three hatches opened up to the inside of the tank, but they were all locked with heavy padlocks. We climbed down, discouraged. The oversize ten-centimeter valve at the bottom also had a large padlock.

"How can we get in there, Opa?" I asked, almost sure that he had some form of bolt cutters or metal-burning torch in his pocket.

"Well, young friends, what do you think? Perhaps you can figure this one out yourselves." He smiled. Eyes twinkling, I know he already had the solution in mind. All three of us climbed back up on top and examined every inch of the hatches. Back down, we studied the drain valve. Everything looked impossible. I even found a giant rock and tried to punch a hole in the heavy gauge metal without even putting much of a dent in it.

"Solving a problem sometimes requires looking at it from a different direction. Would you like a hint?"

I tried to be stubborn and solve it, but Hannah looked at him with her innocent, blue girl eyes.

"Please, Opa, give us a hint!"

Knowing he could not resist that pleading look, he laughed with his head back, took a deep breath, and said, with a coy look of his own, "How many places do they keep petrol on a truck?"

In a flash, I realized we had been looking only at the locked tank. "The engine has to run on something! Here!" I pointed, running to the front of the truck. "Here is the smaller tank that the truck runs on." Sure enough, the tank right beside the driver's door had no lock. I took the cap off and looked in.

"How do we get it out of there, Opa? I guess we could crawl under and get it from the fuel line that runs to the engine. The one we clamped on the equipment truck," I suggested.

"Certainly a possibility, Henry, but let me show you an easier way. First, we need a container to catch the gas." With good fortune we found an empty gas can in the boot of the Daimler. "Here we learn the scientific part. Have you ever heard of a syphon?" We shook our heads. With that, he rummaged around in his coat and found the clear plastic tube where he had kept water. One end threaded into the tank until we could hear it splash in the petrol, the other end Opa held up high.

"Remember something very important, my young friends. Some people use their mouths to try and suck the petrol up the hose to get the syphon started. Do not ever do that. Petrol is toxic and if it gets into your lungs, it will make you very sick. So here is how you do it." Wiping his fingers on a greasy part of the truck, he pinched the plastic hose as close as possible to the open petrol cap and slid his fingers upward until you could see the green liquid rising in the plastic hose. Lowering the high end into the gas can, the petrol began to dribble out of the tube. To our surprise, the dribble soon became a steady stream.

"See, it can seem like magic. The weight of the petrol in the lower end of the hose pulls petrol from the tank, which is higher. It will continue to suck it out until it empties the tank. Presto! *'Take my advice,'*" he quoted. *"It will add years to your life. I'm writing out clear directions to the way of wisdom, I'm drawing a map to the right road. I don't want you to end up in a dead end, or waste time making wrong turns."*

In a very short time, the can filled up to the cap. While Opa pinched the hose, I emptied it into the car three times until the gas needle on the dashboard indicated the tank was almost full.

With a giant whoop, we all climbed back into our lovely vehicle and were on our way. The next big whoop came when we spotted the sign for Osnabrück. A left turn and it looked like we were home free. Almost. We still had to get across the border. They would have gates and guards. Seventy more kilometers and we would have been in Holland , but the Gestapo intervened.

On a straight, smooth road you can see a long way ahead. Three military vehicles were parked on the highway. A roadblock. In a spot where the road went through a gully with high banks on each side. It looked like the end of the road for us.

"Well, my young trio, we have another challenge. Duck down so they can't see you until the last minute and hold on tight. We are going to try to swerve past them on the high bank." Then Opa shouted out, *"Save us, mighty God, and help us with your strong right hand, that those you love may be delivered."*

Two soldiers were waving us down. Opa slowed down as if he were going to stop. I peeked out the side window, sure that Grandfather had probably thought through our situation and was convinced they were not expecting us in a classy sports car. When I looked over at him, Opa had somehow popped on aviator sunglasses and a tweed driving cap. He looked dapper. Five hundred meters rolled quickly down to three, then two. Still, the soldiers were not pointing guns, or looking nervous.

Suddenly, as we drifted and almost stopped, a roar from the mighty Daimler exploded from the tailpipe. The car jumped forward like a gazelle. Wheeling to the left, the car rose up the banked side of the road. Right at the peak, when it felt like we were going airborne, a quick twist and Opa whipped the car back down to the road. A mighty bump as we bottomed out and sprayed sparks behind us. The acceleration pushed us all the way back in our seats. Shouts, orders, and even bullets whipped the wind in our wake but we were long gone.

Zero to one hundred kilometers per hour in six seconds is what that mighty twelve-cylinder engine could do. Exactly what Opa told me later. By the time I could pry my eyes open and look at the speedometer, we were zooming along at one hundred and twenty kilometers an hour. And Opa was laughing like I had never seen him laugh before. Twisting backward, I could see that, way back in the distance, two of the military vehicles were on the road trying to chase us down. Seeing the concerned look on my face, Opa brought his laughter down to a chuckle.

"Not a chance, not a chance." Over the roar of the mighty engine, he yelled, "Look at what else this wonderful vehicle can do! It is called an electric overdrive. Not too many vehicles have them, but … watch this." With that, he reached over and flipped a switch on the console. Vroom … as if someone had put rocket fuel in our tank. The roar settled down to a purr. Faster and faster we went till we were a blur on the landscape. The wind whipping around like a tornado. Nobody would catch us now.

Hannah's face paled to white, emphasizing how big and blue her eyes were. Hans had gotten over his fright and now was enjoying the speed of our vehicle with the fences, light poles, and farmhouses flashing by. The speedometer quivered at around 140 kph. Secretly, I thought that if we ever got out of this crazy mess alive, wow, someday I would buy myself a Daimler. Opa still looked like he was having a great time, but the wind noise prevented him from giving his usual pithy commentary and it kept Henry from spouting poetry.

A white sign flashed by. I think it said *Osnabrück, 15 Kilometers.* At 140 kilometers per hour. Hmm, the numbers in my head bounced around trying to calculate how long that would take, but by the time the answer started to surface, Opa slowed down and the next sign read "Welcome to Osnabrück." The highway narrowed and very quickly we were starting to see some traffic. We turned into a narrow side street, made a few more turns, and stopped in front of what looked to be an abandoned warehouse.

"Vilka gave us this address, a safe house for those trying to get into Holland," Opa announced. "Henry, jump out and open that garage door for us and shut it behind us quickly, before someone recognizes the car."

It came down pretty smoothly, but someone might have seen us pull in. As the door closed, Hannah whispered, "Grandfather, will we be safe here?"

We could't see it, but we heard his cheerful chuckle. "There is no safe place in all of Germany without the Lord, my sweet girl, but, *'The name of the Lord is a strong fortress; the godly run to him and are safe.'"*

Out came the flashlight and our surroundings appeared around us. A front door to the left with what looked like an abandoned office, two truck-size garage doors in the front, and a workbench with one exit door along the back. Our sweet ride sat in the first bay, clicking softly as the engine cooled. I wished we were still zooming toward Holland at 140 kph. No worries. Our grandfather knew what he was doing. He looked around the dusty garage.

"Hans, you peek out that window and let us know if you hear anything or if someone tries to get in."

Opa headed for the exit door and began pushing on it. For sure, it had not been opened in many years. With three of us shoving, it finally screeched open. We found ourselves in a walled-in courtyard littered with dirt, leaves, and debris. No exit. This did not look like a "safe house," and I wondered why the door had been marked "exit." Opa began walking the perimeter and soon stopped at a section in the wall which seemed a bit different in color. Reaching for his Swiss Army Knife, he opened the blade and slipped it into the crack. "Aha," he breathed. "Look what we have here children." With that, the panel opened, revealing a flight of stairs leading up.

Hans came running into the courtyard. "Trucks, big trucks, loaded with soldiers and tanks," he whispered. "They are driving down the street. Some have stopped and are getting out."

"Quick, get inside and help me close this door," hissed Grandfather. The four of us pushed on the hidden door to the courtyard and managed to get it shut. "They will know we have been here because of the car. The secret door will keep them baffled for a short while but we must keep moving."

Up the staircase we climbed and Hans pulled the door at the top of the stairs closed behind us. Ahead, up another flight of stairs, a door opened into a clean, cheerful apartment with light coming in the windows, bright curtains, comfortable furniture, and a small kitchen. With even food and drinks on the counter, I knew someone had been expecting us.

"Yes, this is more like it. Vilka and her mother are truly virtuous women for they are *'like a merchant's ship, bringing food from a long way away.'* Come, my young friends, let us thank the Lord for the food. We can feast while I plan for our next escape, for *'A few crusts of bread with someone you love is much better than a feast with someone you hate.'*" We prayed and, with that, we opened baskets of rolls, smoked fish, fruit, and drinks, and we began filling our stomachs.

No time for a regular meal, the Commandant was on the move. Now nobody would be safe from his wrath. He grabbed a crust of bread and some cheese from a left-over plate on his desk and stomped out the door. Still red-faced from a recent tirade, the head of the Gestapo finally took decisive action to capture those spies. His driver already had his military vehicle waiting; they drove away, headed for the last sighting near Osnabrück. Two Gestapo agents on motorcycles followed behind, not knowing the danger ahead as they roared out of Munster toward the Dutch border.

Escape Eight

"SMART IS BETTER THAN DUMB"

The Journal of Henry Gutmann
Osnabrück, Germany - September 1939

Watching somebody think is boring, but we had to watch our grandfather do it often. He told us he was making a plan. I decided it was like watching wisdom at work. Opa always talked a lot about wisdom. I am sure he used wisdom to figure out how we were going to escape again. Waiting is hard to do when you're bored. There was nothing to do in the small apartment. No books, no magazines, no puzzles or games. We had been warned not to be seen. Peeking very carefully out a dormer window on the third floor, we noticed that each roof of the houses across the street was set close to the next. Down in the narrow streets, military vehicles and squads of soldiers were going house-to-house. It was only a matter of time before they found our hideout. It was hard to believe they were all looking for *us*. For some reason, their leaders were convinced we were the enemy. An old man and three kids. They were deceived. But, I guessed, they were all obeying orders.

Under the pressure of waiting, Hans, Hannah, and I began to be drawn back into fear. When our hearts slowed enough to think about where we were, hunted by the entire Nazi machine, it was frightening.

"I want to go home," wept Hannah, tears running down her face and spilling off her chin. "Henry, are my parents alive? Will I ever see them again?" Hans patted her on the shoulder.

I decided to apply one of Opa's bits of wisdom. *"A cheerful heart is good medicine.'"* I said.

I thought of a wonderful memory of when we visited Opa's set of rooms in downtown Munich. "Hannah, there is no way to answer those questions. The only thing we can do is live today, believing the best and rejecting the worst. When Hans and I first got to know Opa was when our parents allowed us to spend

FOAM, TAPE & A GECKO?

the night in his apartment. It was so full of every kind of tool, device, and widget you can imagine. Drawers, jars, and bins overflowing with grommets and fasteners. It was amazing. I remember the view from his tiny third-

floor window. It looked out right on the main square, where even late at night there was always busy traffic. Even now I can remember him looking over my shoulder and saying, *"'Do you hear Lady Wisdom calling? She is raising her voice. She's taken her stand in the main square, at the busiest intersection. Right in the middle of the city where the traffic is thickest,'"* I looked to see if Hannah was listening, and continued, *"'she shouts, You—I'm talking to all of you, everyone out here on the streets! Listen, don't be foolish—learn good sense! You dummies—shape up! Don't miss a word of this—I'm telling you how to live well, I'm telling you how to live right.'"*

Jumping to his feet, Opa shouted, "I know, I know exactly what we will do!" Looking furtively at the window in this apartment, he lowered his voice to a whisper.

"Sorry, my young friends, I forgot we were hiding here in the loft. Come look out the window. See how they have built the houses so close to each other that you can actually step from one roof to the next? We can escape by going along the roofs till we can find a way down. It is almost dark and nobody is going to be looking up at the roof anyway."

Hannah wiped her tears while all of us crowded around the window to see if it was really possible.

"But Opa," whispered Hannah, "these roofs are so steep and the shingles are slate and very smooth. I am sure we will slide right off, fall to the ground, and die."

"Not if I can help it," quipped Opa with a wink. "Have you ever heard of a creature called a gecko?" We all shook our heads. "Aha, they are a type of lizard that can actually walk on the ceiling because of the special pads on their feet. God designed them in a way that they actually stick to the surface they are walking on. Come help me." With that, he rummaged around in his coat until he found a pair of scissors and a box of single-edge razor blades and a roll of heavy tape. He began pulling the cushions off the couch.

"Hans, you and Henry start cutting the fabric off of these cushions. Hannah, you can take the scissors and start cutting the tape into strips about as long as your forearm." As she started peeling off the tape, I looked at Opa and held up one of the orange cushions we had been sitting on. They were not new by any stretch, but they still looked good.

"Yes, yes, Henry, cut that fabric off, we need the foam inside." He laid the foam pads out on the floor and started tracing around our hands and feet with a stubby pencil, also from his pocket. Using the saw blade in his Swiss Army Knife, he began cutting the shapes of mittens and shoe inserts. Hannah looked over at me as she and Hans were cutting strips of tape. There was real doubt in her eyes. I could see her thinking *"This is the craziest idea I have ever heard. Are we really going to climb around on slate roofs? Like geckos?"*

"Opa," I said, shaking my head, "is this trick really going to work?! I know the leather soles on our shoes will be like snow skis. Even if we had rubber sneakers, I think we would slide off."

"Here, look," said Opa, with that mischievous twinkle in his eye. He held up a foam mitten close to my eyes. "Do you see all those microscopic chambers? They are like the suction cups God designed on the pads of a gecko's feet." He smiled and wiggled his eyebrows up and down. I rolled my eyes up toward the ceiling and imagined the four of us climbing upside down like lizards. Well ... it had to be the craziest idea yet, but Opa had never let us down.

"Lizards," I muttered under my breath and kept cutting.

"Yes, lizards," said Opa cheerfully. "They are one of God's most amazing creatures. There are about five thousand varieties of lizards on the planet. Some can catch flies with their tongues. And they can live anywhere they want. God tells us that, *'It is easy to catch a lizard with your hands, but it still lives in kings' palaces.'*"

"Hello, gecko, I think I hear an echo," mocked Hans.

We looked ridiculous. Taking turns, we had taped foam mittens on each of our hands and feet, with strips of foam around our knees too. Hans started sticking his tongue in and out and making crawling motions he thought a lizard would make. Hannah asked if we would be needing a tail. But none of that bothered Opa. He went to the window again and looked out. The sun had set and darkness creeped along the rooftops, with the chimney pots painting grey striped shadows across the shingles.

"I think it is time, team." Grandfather reached out and turned off the light. Dusk still gave everything outside the window a grey cast, like the old photographs of my parents.

He whispered, "Here is the plan. Hans, you go first since you are the most agile. You must lead the way. See if you can work your way toward a place where we can climb down away from the street where the soldiers are. Hannah, you go next. You follow him."

"I am seriously afraid of heights," she argued quietly with her head down. "I don't think I can do it."

"You must, dear one," said Opa, kneeling in front of her and taking her foam-mittened hands in his. "We are so close to the Dutch border where there is freedom and safety. I am an old man. It doesn't matter what happens to me. But you, Hans, and Henry still have your lives ahead of you. You must live." I noticed that tears began to form in his eyes. "You must be able to tell the truth of the terrible things that have been done in this country. You must warn your children and their children to never let this happen again." With that said, he wiped his eyes and strode to the window.

"Henry, you will be next, and I will follow at the end. Here is what to remember, friends. Don't look down. Keep three contacts with the roof at all times. Only move one hand or one foot at a time. I assure you, you will not fall. Now, the time has come. Let's go. "*'Wisdom is calling us, she has lifted up her voice from the rooftop, from the heights beside the way. Where paths meet, she takes her stand.'*"

I would not have believed it had I not been watching with my own eyes. Hans put his first foot out the window onto the slanted roof. Then his right hand, followed by his left hand, and finally his other foot. He looked like a lizard clinging to the side of the steeply slanted roof. Slowly he began moving, first to one side and climbing up toward the peak. Pale-faced and trembling slightly, Hannah turned sideways and eased her foot out onto the slates. She moved much slower than Hans, but gradually, one hand, one foot at a time, she moved out of our sight.

Now it was my turn. Without looking down, I took a deep breath and swung my leg over the windowsill. I turned and put my weight on that foot. I claimed to be an experienced climber.

Trees, rocks, buildings, and ropes in the gym were all easy for me.

I could clearly remember trying to sneak out one night by climbing out a dormer window onto a slate roof. I only got one foot onto the slate when I realized it was not going to work. The roof was too steep, shoes too slick, so when my first foot slipped, I collapsed back into the room. No more sneaking out for me.

The fear this time was as real as I remembered, but I was also amazed that my foot clung to the slate just like Opa had said it would! Moving cautiously, I did feel a bit like a lizard, only much slower. We were all in line, headed toward the roof peak. Hans, followed by Hannah, then me, and I assumed Opa was following behind. Not looking down definitely had to be the best thing to do.

Suddenly something happened that either Opa had not considered or had hoped would not happen. A damaged shingle broke loose. Hannah's foot slipped and a stone shingle skidded down the roof, zipped between my hands, and, gathering speed, flew off the edge somewhere behind me. We all froze. I heard Hannah whimpering. Reaching up, I pushed her foot up.

"Here, Hannah, push against my hand and keep going."

Behind me, I could hear Opa murmuring encouragement. *"You will keep walking safely and your foot will not slip. When you rest, you will not be afraid; when you lie down, your sleep will be sweet. Don't be afraid of sudden fear, or of the wicked ones who are after us. For the LORD will be your confidence and will keep your foot from slipping."*

Slowly we started moving again. After what seemed like days of climbing, we gathered on a flat spot at the base of a cluster of chimneys. We all breathed a huge sigh of relief. Hannah, with dry tear tracks on her cheeks, held her hand over her heart and seemed to be drawing strength from somewhere beyond herself—or perhaps from the words that Opa had been quoting. Finally, with a shuddering sigh, she asked, "Opa, where do the words come from that you recite with such confidence? They seem to have some kind of magic in them." I glanced over at Hans knowingly. He had a smile on his face, sure of what was to follow.

"It is nothing like magic, dear Hannah," Opa said. "Magic is only an illusion. It is a way of fooling the eye, making it appear as if something supernatural has happened. It is just tricks. These words are miraculous. They are the very words written by King Solomon, the wisest person who ever lived. But even more, they are 'breathed,' inspired by God himself."

"They are mostly from the book of Proverbs in the Bible," Hans added with pride in his voice. "Grandfather memorized the entire book. Forward, backward, and anywhere in between."

"Well," chuckled Opa, "not the backward part. That would reverse the meaning and we would not want to follow that." Very seriously, he added, "However, written within its pages we find the most valuable wisdom, which will keep us from getting into trouble, and when we do, it can help us get out in miraculous ways."

"But Opa," Hannah said. (It pleased me to hear her calling him Opa. I knew she was beginning to like him and trust him too.) "It seems to me that you and all of us are in a lot of trouble right now. How did we get in it and how can we get out?"

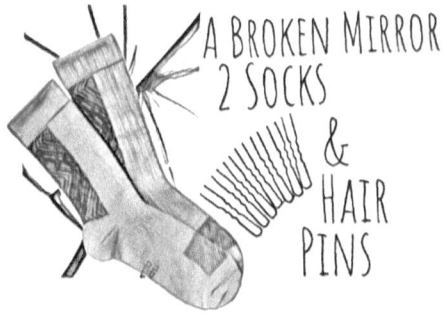

She looked earnestly at him, but somehow with the confidence that he would provide an answer and a solution. What none of us knew at that point was that the next challenge would require some of Hannah's hairpins, two socks full of sand, and a piece of broken mirror.

The road to Osnabrück was empty of all traffic when rain started to fall. The two Gestapo agents on motorcycles were having a hard time keeping up with the Commandant's car in the heavy downpour. But there was no slowing down. Anger in his heart kept him from thinking clearly. He could only yell at his driver to go faster. He would not be made a fool by an old man and two children. They would be captured, returned to Munich, and tortured to discover what they knew. The Commandant knew how to extract information through torture. No one could keep secrets from him.

Journal One

Escape Nine

"GLAD IS BETTER THAN MAD"

The Journal of Henry Gutmann
Hiding in Osnabrück, Germany - September 1939

Getting off the roof turned out to be one of the easiest things we had done in days. We crawled like lizards, or geckos if you want to be more accurate, all the way to the other side of the house. The shingles cooperated and stayed in place. Our gecko pads clung to the shingles and we all safely climbed onto a deck that faced a tiny walled garden. From the deck, a metal ladder designed to be a fire escape allowed us to climb down to the ground. The small but well-tended garden appeared to be Vilka's work. A stone bench, pots with cheerful flowers, plants, and two miniature stone gnomes leaning toward each other as if almost kissing but frozen in time. It made me think a bit about Hannah. She was even cuter than the girl gnome getting ready to …well … sad that she would never get a kiss from her stone boyfriend.

"Henry, come on!" whispered Hans. "You can't be dreaming out here in the garden. Opa said we need to get moving." Peeling my gecko hands and feet off, I started helping Hannah with hers. A razor from one of the boxes Opa carried in his pockets helped cut the tape. Within minutes we were walking toward the only doorway that opened out of the garden. I patted the girl gnome on her head on the way past. I blushed a bit when I noticed Hannah watching.

From inside the house, we could hear loud music, and light streamed out the curtained window. Hans, a bit taller, could look in; I had to stand on tiptoe. I could see three young men sitting around a table cluttered with beer bottles. It looked like a tavern or a restaurant. I could hear an intense conversation going on between the three men. Faces close together, eyes squinted almost shut, voices low. Something important laced the words.

Grandfather walked up to the door and opened it like he owned the place, typical of his sense of confidence. As he opened the door, he turned and motioned for us to wait against the wall, held a finger to his lips, and slipped into the room. I looked in the window again. Opa stood behind the counter talking to the woman washing glasses. Abruptly, one man jumped to his feet, shoved his chair back, and yelled at Grandfather. Crash! The chair hit the wall as he confronted Opa with an angry red face.

"Hey!" he taunted. "You stupid old man! You better get out of here before you get into trouble. We don't like to be interrupted. Get your decrepit carcass moving!"

I really wanted to rush in and protect my grandfather, but that didn't make sense. Three large men against one teenager. It would not end well. I should have known there was nothing to worry about. Grandfather smiled at the angry young man, opened both hands wide, bowed his head with respect, and responded in a gentle voice.

"My sincere apologies, gentlemen. I had not been informed you were meeting this evening. My friend Vilka ..." At the mention of her name the angry man pulled back. "... has been preparing the way for us. I am sure she will explain," finished Grandfather. Grumbling, the red-faced aggressor backed away, picked his fallen chair off the floor, and sat back down with his comrades. Giving one last angry look at Grandfather and the girl, he resumed his discussion with the other two men. Relieved, I don't know why I still worried about my grandfather getting into trouble. He had some sort of special spirit that hovered around him.

In a moment he leaned out and beckoned for us to come inside. The door opened into a storeroom in the back of the restaurant, and we could hear the music and the men still grumbling at the intrusion. The woman working behind the counter stepped in and motioned for us to follow her. We knew it was Gretel, Vilka's mother, the moment we saw her. Chubby and short like a giant sweet roll, with cheeks as rosy as the little gnomes in her garden, she smiled so wide it puffed her cheeks and crinkled her eyes almost shut.

"Please forgive my son and his friends," said Gretel. "Everyone is fearful of the Gestapo and is trying to hide from their cruel punishment. They're suspicious of everyone."

"Gosh, Gretel we didn't know he was your son. Opa, I thought that he and his two friends were going to beat you up. Were you scared?"

"Not a bit, Henry," he chuckled. *"A hot-tempered person stirs up conflict, but one slow to anger calms everything down,"* he quoted. "But Gretel, you do know that if that young man does not listen to instruction, one day his anger will get him into trouble because *A person who does not control his temper is like a city without any defenses."*

"Oh, young people, how precious your grandfather is," she deflected. "So proud and brave to rescue you all from the evil one." Immediately, she started with Hannah, giving out hugs for as long as we would hold still. "We have prayed for safe passage and now see that God has answered our prayers by bringing you this far." Pulling us into her kitchen, grabbing food from her icebox and pantry, encouraging us to eat. "Tell me now of your adventures!"

"Oh, Gretel, it has been so scary and wonderful," mumbled Hannah with her mouth full. "Opa rescued me on the train, then we got captured by a crazy man who loaned us his car that went so fast as we escaped from the Gestapo. We had to hide in your apartment and climbed out on the roof like geckos and now we are looking for a place to hide from the Nazis who are trying to capture us … but every time Opa has some clever plan to help us escape and …"

"Wait, wait," laughed Opa. "We don't have the time to tell the whole story. Gretel, you have been such a wonderful angel to help us. Do you know how we can get out of here and back on the road to the border? I think they have posted a countrywide alert to find us and return us to Munich for processing and send us … well, you know." He paused because we all knew what he was going to say. It would not be wise for anyone to say out loud or even think about what they were doing to captives, especially for Hannah's sake because her parents had already been captured and ... well, you know too.

"Yes, I know a place you can hide for a while. Duchess Hildegard von Bismarck is the daughter of Chancellor Otto von Habsburg. The Nazis, and especially Hitler, hate the Habsburgs because they organized the Resistance to undermine his authority. Two years ago they abolished all royalty, but they still treat the Duchess with respect because of how beloved she is among the people. She used to be the wealthiest woman in our town, but the Nazis have taken all her family's wealth. Her house is right across the street and she secretly sympathizes with the Resistance and tries to help where she can." Gretel leaned in closer and lowered her voice. "She is also fearful because her mother was part Jewish and that is all it takes. The Führer has said even one drop of Jewish blood will pollute the Arian race and must be eliminated."

"How can we get to this woman's house, Gretel? We don't know where to go," said Hans, the most nervous of us, wanting specific details.

"That, my friend, is the easy part. We have a lorry that makes deliveries from the back of our shoppe and you can ride in it to the side entrance of her house where we make deliveries."

"That is good to know," said Hans, quite relieved.

"The only thing you need to be careful of is Duchess Hildegard's sister, Helmtrud. She is most troublesome. She won't reveal you to the Nazis because she hates them, but she hates everyone. She is quite argumentative."

"Aha, a Proverbs Nine kind of woman," said Opa knowingly.

Of course, Hannah had to ask, "What is a Proverbs Nine woman, Opa?"

Opa chuckled. "Well, Hannah, there are two kinds of women spoken of in Proverbs Nine. The wise woman who calls out from the highest places of the town, *'Everybody who needs to learn, come and see me!' To people who don't have any sense she says, 'Leave your foolish ways and you will live; follow the path that makes sense.'* She is like our friend, Gretel, here."

"Oh hush, Grandfather, you embarrass me," Gretel said, swatting him with a dish towel.

"Or the other kind," he continued, "is called foolish, and is a loud, argumentative woman. *'She sits at the door of her house, yelling, "Hey, come and see me! We can steal some good food and drink. No one will ever know!" But those who stop in don't know about those who died listening to her advice.'*"

"I had forgotten that you had memorized the book of wisdom," Gretel said as she nodded. "Well, for sure don't try and argue with Helmtrud. She makes fun of anyone who believes in the Creator."

"Ah, yes, that would be true to form," said Grandfather. "It goes on to say, *'Whoever argues with a mocker invites insults; whoever rebukes the wicked will be abused. Do not argue with mockers or they will hate you.'*"

"You, friends, pay attention to what your grandfather has to say," Gretel warned. "It is always wisdom from The Book."

"Ok, enough talking," said Hans nervously. "We need to get somewhere safe."

Gretel suddenly became all business. First, she pointed to the chubby van driver standing by the storeroom door. "This is my sweet-loaf husband Oskar. He will drive you to Hildegard's house." Oskar came over and hugged Grandfather without saying anything and Gretel began hugging all of us again while wiping tears with her apron.

"You will be safe, I know you will," she said between tears.

We followed her through the storeroom, out a back door, and into an alley where the delivery van was parked at the end of the lane near the street. Oskar turned to look in the other direction and quickly flattened himself against the wall beside the door. He held his hand out to stop us from coming any further. A stack of crates hid our view of the other end of the alley.

With his face pinched by worry, he held his finger to his lips and shook his head. "There is a soldier that stepped into the alley to relieve himself. We can't leave now."

Gretel peeked out the door and whispered, "Soldiers have come in the front door and are wanting to search the restaurant for you. I'm afraid they will arrest my son and his friends. You must go now!"

Caught between the search behind and the soldier in front, I didn't know what we were going to do. Hans got a panicked look on his face. Hannah looked at Opa. He looked up, thinking. Don't think too long, Opa. We have got to do something quick! is what I thought.

"I will go talk to him," said Oskar. "Perhaps I can convince him to go somewhere else for his business."

"No," said Grandfather firmly. *"'If you argue with a scoffer, all you get is more arguments.'* Hans," he spoke quietly, "take off one of your socks and fill it halfway with sand from this pile by the door and tie a knot in it. Henry, get down on your hands and knees. Peek around the boxes and tell me exactly what you see. Hannah, I need some of those hairpins I have seen you use to pin up your hair."

Looking around the corner on my hands and knees, I whispered to Opa. "I can see a soldier about thirty feet away, standing with his back to us, facing the wall at the end of the alley. He has a machine gun strapped to his back." Knowing my grandfather was coming up with a plan, I tried to describe everything exactly as I saw it. "It looks like his belt is unbuckled and his pants are down around his hips."

Opa, already moving before I turned back around, had found a broken piece of a mirror in one of his pockets somewhere. He held it in one hand with the knotted sock filled with sand in the other. Reaching beyond the protective crates, Opa held the broken mirror out into a patch of sunlight. He reflected the light down the alley to the wall right above the soldier's face.

I remembered, one time years ago, watching our pet cat trying to catch a spot of sunlight reflected from my father's watch.

Opa moved the light spot in a quivering circle on the wall and the soldier looked up and started following with his eyes exactly like our pet cat. Also very catlike, Opa stepped out from behind the crates and, in three strides, reached the soldier and swung the sock full of sand in a giant arc. With a thump, the sock bounced off the back of the soldier's hypnotized head. He dropped like a bag. Yup, just like a bag of sand.

"Oskar," Grandfather ordered in a hoarse whisper, "open the back doors and start the van. Hannah, you get into the front seat. Quick, boys, he won't be out forever. He is only stunned. Come and help me drag the soldier and load him into the back."

This German soldier and his gun were extra heavy and it took all three of us to drag him to the back doors and load him in.

"Hannah," I called out, "don't look back. This soldier lost his britches while we were dragging him down the alley."

"Eww, gross," she said, and started laughing.

"Let's go, Oskar!" yelled Grandfather as he slammed the door shut. "Hans, tie his shoelaces together while I tape his arms and put some on his mouth in case he wakes up."

"What are you laughing about, Hannah?" asked Hans.

"I just wondered who ordered a naked German soldier and where we were going to deliver him." Hannah got Hans laughing with that, and pretty soon Oskar and Opa were laughing too.

Still laughing, Opa asked Hannah for the hairpins and started working them into the bullet chamber of the soldier's rifle.

"This soldier will only try to shoot this gun once, and it will be useless with hairpins all twisted into the firing mechanism."

Oskar liked that, laughing even louder.

"Drive us out into the country for this delivery, Oskar. I know you can find a convenient place to dump him." Soon Oskar pulled off on a dirt side road by a winding creek. Getting the soldier out turned out to be the easy part. I thought it funny imagining him waking up and finding himself with no pants on, and even funnier thinking about him trying to shoot his gun, only to have it blow up in his hands.

As we eased back into town, I could not help thinking about the adventure showing up next. I will tell you that the next rescue was very cleverly executed by Opa with a grand piano, three pieces of felt, an antique hinge, and a tiny bottle of hair oil.

Signs for Osnabrück said they only had 17 km to go but the Commandant did not take any chances. The rain had stopped. Radio reception was now coming in clear. He was still very angry. "Give me a report! I want news of the old man and the two boys," shouted the Commandant into the mouthpiece.

"I am sorry, sir," came the answer. "We found the Daimler car they were driving but, again, it seems as if they have vanished into thin air." The voice came across nervously, "I have two entire squadrons searching every street and alley in Osnabrück. We will find them soon. I am sure of it."

That report did not calm his anger one bit.

Escape Ten

"Kind is better than Cruel"

The Journal of Henry Gutmann
In the Duchess's palace, Osnabrück Germany - September 1939

When Oskar's van turned into the side street behind Hildegard's house, we had to come to a complete stop. The street, completely jammed with military vehicles, made it clear we were not getting anywhere near that house.

Oskar seemed undeterred. "Quick, let's assemble these cardboard boxes and I will cart you over on my hand truck." Opa, efficient with the tape and his Swiss Army Knife, stepped over to three large refrigerator boxes stacked in the back of the van. They were big enough to hold two people each. I decided that Hannah needed me to keep her from being nervous, so I told Hans to crawl into the box with Opa. It would be a tight fit, but with Oskar's encouragement we squeezed in and he started to seal them up.

"Don't worry about the air, you won't be in there for more than about ten minutes." He was trying to reassure us, but memories of the hot dark cabinet that Hans and I had been locked in for four whole days made me shiver.

Hannah spoke. "Don't worry, Henry, I am nervous too. Are you afraid of tight places?"

"It's a long story," I told her. "Someday if we get out of this mess I will tell you about it." Hans would be sweating it too but he had Opa with him, which was more comforting.

The two-wheel cart banged out the back doors as Oskar slid Hans and Opa out first. Hannah and I waited in the growing heat. We, or I should say *I*, got more nervous. Finally, we heard the rattle of Oskar's hand truck returning. Treating us like valuable furniture, he gently lifted us onto the hand truck and began rolling down the sidewalk to the back door of the Duchess's house. We had been told she was a kind woman.

"And where do you think you are going?" We could hear a German soldier begin to question Oskar with a loud voice.

As cool as an ice cube, he answered, "This is precious cargo, mein Herr. Fine furniture. A royal gift from the Führer himself for the Duchess. She is expecting this delivery." It felt even hotter inside our box. The soldier jiggled the box, causing Hannah and I to slide against each other. Still nervous, I took her hand and whispered, "Don't worry, Oskar will get us there. He is so brave."

Then we were rolling again. Without any other hiccups, we arrived at what I guessed was the side gate. Oskar rang a bell. Only silence. A gate squeaked open and we trundled along a rough path to a smooth floor where Oskar set us down. A quick slice opened the box top and fresh air poured in. It was Opa rescuing us again with his Swiss Army Knife in hand.

"Come, friends, the Duchess is waiting for us. Vilka got word to her that we were coming. She told the Duchess that three Bibles and an Old Testament were arriving." I caught on right away that Hannah had been dubbed the "Old Testament." Looking over at her, I wondered if that made her uncomfortable, but she was so excited to get out of the box that she didn't even notice.

Up a narrow flight of stairs which must have been a servant's entrance, we climbed and squeezed through a narrow door into the back of a large kitchen. Set out on the center table was a spread of food fit for a duchess. Hans was already stuffing his face with chicken, turkey, pickles, and fruit. Talking with a mouthful of food, he waved the turkey leg he had been chewing on toward a most regal-looking lady with grey hair piled up on her head in an elegant sweep. "Say hello to Hildegard von Bismarck, the Duchess of …"

The elegant lady's laugh tinkled around the kitchen. "I am the Duchess of nothing right now. They have taken away all royalty status and made us commoners."

She turned serious. "Fortunately, I have my home, but even that is in danger of being confiscated." Smiling again, she gestured toward the food. "For now, we still have a roof over our heads and plenty of food to eat. Let us enjoy it while we can."

"Ah yes," spoke Grandfather, "but we thank you so much for your generosity, your highness. We are told about women like you in The Book. *'A person who gives freely gains even more.'* And also *'A diligent hand will rule.'*"

"Now, let us give thanks for this abundance before we start stuffing our faces." He looked over his glasses at Hans, who paused with the turkey leg halfway to his mouth.

"Great Father and giver of every gift, *'your fruit is better than solid gold and your harvest is better than silver.'* We know that our host has honored you with the firstfruits of her entire harvest, and you have filled her barns. Her vats have overflowed with your abundance. We thank you for it all. Amen." After clearing his throat, Grandfather nodded toward Hans. "You may continue, my hungry friend."

After our abundant feast, the Duchess ushered us into a high-ceilinged sitting room with a gaping fireplace at one end and a lovely white grand piano at the other. We noticed hardly any other furniture scattered around the large room, but we sat on the few velvet chairs and listened as the Duchess shared stories of her own childhood growing up in Habsburg Castle. What fun adventures she had as a child running up and down the stairs in the towers and hiding in the cave-like cellars! It all changed when Hitler came into power.

"All of our land and wealth was confiscated by the Nazi regime. Even our families were divided by the war. We have not been together since. But God has been good and preserved the lives of my sister and me."

I thought about my parents, wondering if they had been preserved. A wave of sadness came over me. What Hannah asked next made it worse.

"Miss Duchess," asked Hannah, "aren't you real sad that your family has been separated and all your castles and land have been taken away from you?"

The Duchess looked sad for a moment. "I grieved when many of my family and our friends were executed for helping the Resistance, but everything we had belonged to the Lord. He gives and He takes away. His name is blessed forever."

"But what did you do all day, hanging around a fancy castle with all the gold you could hold, Duchy?" asked Hans, sounding a bit cocky.

Tinkling across the room, her silver laughter raised pink in her cheeks, making her look girlish. "No, Hans, our family was not that way. Like you, we believe the words of The Book and from those of us to whom much had been given, much was expected. We had no option. What does the Word say about generosity, Opa?" She nodded with respect at my grandfather.

"Oh my." Opa's smile crinkled his eyes almost shut with pleasure. *"The whole town celebrates when generous people are successful."*

It was obvious to me that the Duchess was very kind to allow us into her home.

"We certainly thank you for your kindness." Trying to lighten the mood, Opa pointed to the grand piano in the center of the room.

"Duchess, I remember hearing about the piano concerts you would host at your castle. I would love to hear you play a song for us. Perhaps softly, so we do not attract too much attention."

She laughed and wiggled her fingers as if she were playing. "Alas, it will be a very silent concert, my dear friends. Before the war started, we sent the internal frame off to the Steinway factory in Hamburg to repair a crack in the soundboard. Alas, bombs destroyed that section of the factory and my piano parts with it."

"What a shame, Duchess." Grandfather walked over to the elegant instrument. "I guess you could pretend to play and we could pretend to listen." Everyone laughed at the idea. Lifting the lid, he peered in. It was miraculous that he did. At that very moment, loud banging at the door startled us all. "Quick, help me move the piano to the dark corner of the room." Not sure what or why we were going to do that, but nobody asked.

"No, wait," whispered the Duchess, "you cannot move it. There are no wheels on it and it will make a terrible screeching noise."

The banging on the door was even louder.

"Duchess," whispered Opa, "you go to the door. Oskar, start folding the boxes and get them ready to take back to the truck. We will be fine. Now, Henry and Hans, help me lift." In his hands Opa had already produced some pieces of felt and a tiny bottle.

"Hannah, we will lift each leg of the piano and you must squirt some of this hair oil on each felt piece and set it on the floor under the foot." I was convinced he had lost his mind this time, yet in the minutes it took us to complete the three legs, I had figured it out. The piano could not be that heavy without the soundboard. With each foot set on a square of oiled felt, it slid across the marble floor like on ice. We could hear loud voices coming up the stairs. Once in the shadow of the corner,

Opa held the lid open and helped each of us in turn crawl into the empty space. He climbed in last and, although it was a bit smaller than the boxes, we all fit with the lid closed tight. I had to admit it, my heart started hammering like a kettle drum. We could hear Oskar in the room, whistling as he packed up the boxes and then headed down to take them back to his truck. My head felt like a bomb ready to explode. Not only was I lying in a very confined, dark space again, but my imagination started running wild. How did the Gestapo know to come looking for us? What would Oskar say if they asked which furniture he delivered? Would they see the oily stripes on the floor left by moving the piano? Could they hear my heart beating like a machine gun? Hannah, lying beside me, could probably hear it. She reached out for my hand and took it in hers. I wasn't sure if it helped slow my heart down or made it beat faster.

Much stomping, along with the slamming of cabinets and closet doors, went on for almost two hours. Finally, they seemed to be gone. Opa rustled and lifted the lid a tiny sliver. In his hand he held a square tube. He held one end up to his eye and the other end a few millimeters above the edge. Ahh, I had seen that before. It looked like a miniature version of the periscope they had on submarines. Opa could see out of the tiny crack made by lifting the lid a wee bit. We heard a soft "shhh" as he lowered the lid.

"They left a sentry behind to see if we came out of some secret hiding place," he whispered. "We must lie very still until they go." The "ticktock" of the grandfather clock next to the piano made it seem much longer. Finally, we heard the "ticktock" of the Duchess's high-heeled shoes.

"Well, they have all gone. I will play a celebration march on my piano." She pretended to play the keys and one of the hammers on the inside hit Hans on the nose. He tried to squash a sneeze and only succeeded in passing gas.

"Oh, get us out of here now," I said in a choked voice as the Duchess burst out in her tinkling laugh while lifting the lid.

"Help! We need gas masks," I yelped.

"Oh, be quiet," mumbled Hans. "It was just an accident."

"Are you sure they have all gone, your highness?" I tried to ask. "That was a close call."

"Duchess," Grandfather said while bowing low, "your hospitality and kindness have been severely tested by our presence here. If we had been found, you would have been implicated and punished as severely as ourselves. You know that *'A kindhearted woman receives honor.'*"

"You are kind to say so, my friend," she said as she reached out to touch him on the shoulder, "but there is not much honor in being hounded by this government. We will do well to survive and pray that the honor will be shared later."

"Yes, my dear Duchess, but the Word continues, *'If you are kind, you will be rewarded, but cruel people only harm themselves.'* We are grateful for whatever crumbs you have shared with us, friend."

The accommodations were not crumbs, they were way more luxurious than we had grown up with, and we all slept well. So many adventures happened each day, I had to jot down a few notes, hoping that when the time came to tell the story I would not forget.

Meanwhile, Hans snored in the elegant four-poster bed with a canopy over the top. Nobody could have guessed what our next adventure was to be, nor would they have believed that Opa would rescue us with a bedpan, a handful of pencil shavings, four sticks of chewing gum, a book of matches, and three pairs of shoelaces .

The Commandant was not a kind man. When he wheeled into the garage at Gestapo headquarters in Osnabrück, everyone jumped to attention. He immediately took over the officer's desk and demanded an update.

"Where are they? I want those spies captured now. Are they still in Osnabrück?"

Three local soldiers faced him across the desk. The senior officer stepped forward and bravely gave his report.

"Heil Hitler, Commandant. One report stated they saw four traveling in the Daimler we found in the garage. They must have added a woman to their group of spies. But we have monitored all traffic and only two trucks requesting travel papers have left."

"Show me the travel papers for the trucks. Now! If they have escaped, all of you will suffer greatly." All three men shivered. The Commandant's cruelty was well known.

Escape Eleven

"WORK IS BETTER THAN LAZY"

The Journal of Henry Gutmann
In the Duchess's palace, Osnabrück, Germany -
October 1939

"I have always loved watching and learning from the ants, Hans," said Opa. "They are the most amazing of God's creatures. They are always working. I used to lie on the floor in my mother's kitchen, watching a line of ants who had discovered a crust of bread underneath the legs of our stove. Nobody could find anything on my mother's clean floor. But there it was. Happy ants were breaking bits off and carrying them back to their nest for food during the winter. I laughed at one ant who had bitten off more than he could carry, then struggled to drag it through the tiny hole in the floor where their nest was. He finally had to bite it into smaller pieces. But wise King Solomon respected ants. He said, *'Go to the ant, you slacker! Watch its ways and become wise. Without a leader, boss, or ruler, it collects food in summer, gathering provisions during harvest.'* Yes, those ants were hard workers."

"My great grandfather, Otto von Bismarck, used to quote from the Good Book too," answered the Duchess. "He used that verse about the hinges. What was that one, Opa?"

"Ah, yes, one of my favorites. *A door swings back and forth on its hinges like a slacker turns over on his bed.*"

"Squeak, squeak," squealed Hans, swinging his head back and forth with his eyes shut. Hannah laughed and Opa rolled his eyes toward the ceiling.

"Well," spoke Oskar. "With all due respect, we have some serious work to do. Rolling around in bed won't do it. We need to come up with a plan. We have to talk about how to get Grandfather and these young friends out of Germany and somewhere away from danger. I heard in the tavern that the Commandant of Munster himself has become convinced you are clever spies and has come looking for you personally. His own soldiers in the Gestapo have begun making fun of him behind his back, saying, "Children and doddering old men are more clever than the Führer's right-hand man.""

It surprised me when Hannah spoke up. "Well, Opa is way more clever than that dunderhead. Opa knows how to do everything."

"No, Hannah, I know some things, but what I have learned from the Good Book is more than enough to make me sound wise. We know, *Lazy hands make you poor, but diligent hands bring riches.*"

Unrolling a tube of paper from his pocket, Opa also pulled the map he had found in the truck's glove box, plus three colored pencils, and laid them on top of the piano. Everybody leaned over the map as he ran his finger up the road north toward Holland.

"Our friend Oskar has suggested an idea which will require some work, but if we are going to make it out of Germany hard work will be required." Opa began sketching on the white paper. "He is suggesting that we build a box big enough for this lovely grand piano with also enough room for all of us." He pointed the pencil at us. "Inside the box he can transport us in his truck all the way to the other piano factory in Holland."

"Oh no," I said, shaking my head. "That sounds like too much work and you're not going to get Hans inside any more boxes. I think he is done with tight spaces."

"Don't worry, Henry," Opa said cheerfully. "We will drop you off at the nearest Gestapo headquarters and they can pop you into a four-by-four jail cell. Or perhaps they would give you a brand-new Hitler Youth uniform and send you goose-stepping off down the Bergstrasse, shouting 'Heil Hitler' while giving the Hitler salute." It wasn't funny, but I laughed anyway at the thought of high stepping, like a goose, down the street.

"No, no," said Oskar. "This will be a large box. One side that can open to reveal the piano but with a hidden compartment and a hidden door so you can step out when needed." He grabbed one of Opa's pencils and began sketching a rough schematic on Opa's paper.

"It sounds like a lot of work to me," I mumbled.

"Does anyone have other suggestions that might work?" Opa looked around. The silence was finally broken by Hannah in her whispery voice.

"I heard of a Jewish family that sewed a balloon out of tent material, filled it with helium, and floated across the border at night." Hans snickered, then got quiet at seeing the sad look on Hannah's face, knowing she wished her family had been able to do that.

Opa cleared his throat. "It is a very good idea, Hannah. I heard of the two families who did manage to escape, but we are way too far from the border yet, and a balloon floats very slowly unless you have high winds. It could be dangerous."

"The only other thing I can think of, my Friend," the Duchess said as she looked at my grandfather and crinkled her eyes in a warm smile, "but it would be a smelly way to get out, is to crawl through the city sewer. I know my father extended the tunnels all the way to the edge of town."

I noticed that their eyes stayed connected a long time.

Trying to lighten things up a bit, I rolled my eyes while saying, "Well, it wouldn't smell much worse than being inside the piano with Hans." He gave me a dirty look, but Oskar laughed.

"Look, I have a man who works for me that could paint the piano factory logo on my van. After we loaded you into it, I would drive you to Holland. Perhaps you could escape by boat to Amsterdam."

Oskar looked at Grandfather, the Duchess next, then me, lastly Hans, and finally Hannah. Nobody seemed to disagree.

"Well, Oskar, what will you need?" asked the Duchess, who knew much about getting things done. At that point everyone went to work. For the next few weeks, we carried wood and parts up and down the stairs. The box began to take shape following the drawings on the roll of paper and under Oskar's diligent hand. We stayed away from the windows and couldn't use lights to work at night. Each day we could see significant progress. Only twice did the Gestapo come knocking on the door looking for the "spies." A quick climb into the empty piano kept us hidden when we heard the discussion between Oskar and the soldiers.

"What are you building here?" Loud, as if they were always angry. "You have been doing this for weeks."

"Heil Hitler, Major, a large victory concert is scheduled for the Yuletide and this piano, being one of the finest in Germany, must be repaired and ready. The Duchess has graciously allowed it to be transported and used at the gala event."

"Well, get finished up and clear out of here," he yelled. "We might need this space for war strategy meetings and the rooms for lodging."

I thought about how carefully we cleaned out our rooms each morning, leaving no trace of our presence, and how lightly we slept at night with the fear they could barge in and arrest us at any moment. All of our days were spent cutting, shaping by hand, and screwing the box together. It was a big box. I worried it might not fit into Oskar's truck. Opa worked as hard as anyone, but during times of rest he would sit next to the Duchess and they would talk softly with their heads almost touching. During the entire time, the Duchess cooked, cleaned, carried tools, and spent time teaching Hannah how to knit.

"Winter is coming soon. You will all need mittens, scarves, and toboggans to keep you warm."

Finally, the day came. Oskar left and, the next day, returned with two burly helpers who carried the piano down to the lower level, lifted it into the box, and braced it inside.

"Now, friends, let's try crawling inside." Using a screwdriver, Oskar opened the secret panel on the side below the heavy braces that framed the box. Silently the door swung open and he pointed us to the inside. Hannah took my hand and led the way. Her bravery continually amazed me. Hans was nervous, I could tell, but Opa took him by the shoulder and ushered him inside, bringing up the rear. I was surprised that Oskar had made it roomier than I had imagined; we all climbed in.

A bench ran the width of the box and we were able to sit shoulder to shoulder looking at the panel that separated us from the piano. Unless you took a ruler and measured from the inside of the piano compartment, it was almost impossible to discern the existence of the secret compartment. I had mentioned often that it required a tremendous amount of work to save three kids and an old man, but Oskar reassured me.

"Every life we save is worth it Henry, and you will be able to give testimony to the outside world of the atrocities that are being committed by this mad man and his government."

"This is very nice," said Hannah, squeezing my hand. "From there, Oskar said it would take only one or two hours to Enschede at the border in Holland, then another hour to Amsterdam. It should be easy."

Oskar leaned into the compartment. "That is true, but the road can be rough at times and the Gestapo has many checkpoints. Crossing the border into Holland will be the decisive challenge."

The Duchess handed each of us a basket of food and other items we tucked at our feet under the bench. One item I hoped we didn't need to use was a bedpan. Hans saw it and made a disgusted face.

"Please be safe," the Duchess murmured, reaching out and touching each of us on the cheek, lingering longest on the face of Opa. Tears formed in her eyes as he reached up to lightly touch her hand. "I will be praying for you," she said.

"And I for you, friend," he responded.

"No time to linger," said Oskar abruptly. "It is time to go." The door shut. Some light filtered in through hidden air vents above, but it still was very dark. I could feel Hans shiver next to me.

"No passing gas," I whispered. He responded by punching me in the arm.

We heard the garage door squeal open and the sound of Oskar's truck backing up to the box, then the metal clang of a ramp being lowered from the back of the truck. We felt the box shaking as the men, using dollies, rolled it up into the truck bed. As the back door to the truck slammed, it went completely black.

Blink. A friendly light appeared from Opa's coat and the magnet on the back clicked onto a large bolt holding the door together.

"Well, fellow adventurers, we are on the road again," Opa tossed out cheerfully as the truck began rattling along the streets of Osnabrück toward Enschede. "The generosity of our friend, the Duchess, has been a wonderful blessing."

"Henry," he said as he handed me something that clinked, "these are two bent nails linked together. See if you can figure out how to get them apart. Being able to manipulate things without using your eyes might come in useful someday. Hans, here is a ball of twine I need you to untangle. And Hannah, here are five hand-carved wooden dolls. They are all nested inside each other. If you take them apart, put each one on a finger like a thimble. The challenge is to put them all back together."

I knew Opa was keeping us busy so we would not get bored. It didn't make any sense to me, fiddling with those nails without being able to see, but I did learn something that came in very useful only days later. I tried. I really did. Even though I twisted and turned those two nails every way I could think of, they remained stubbornly linked together.

Hans, on the other hand, said, "Never fear, Mr. Lucky is here. He is untying lots of tricky knots."

"Wait till the light comes on," I mumbled skeptically, "so we can see what kind of crazy tangle you have there."

"These dolls fit together so perfectly, Opa," said Hannah. "Where did you get them?"

"They are made in Russia and are called Matryoshka dolls. It takes much skill to make them."

"And what are you doing in the dark while we play with dolls, Opa?" she said.

"I am sharpening pencils."

Finally, I spoke up. "Opa, my fingers have gotten too cold. I give up. I think you have to unhook these twisted nails."

With a soft chuckle, Opa reached out and put his hands around mine, felt for the tip and the head on each nail, positioned my fingers at the same place and, with a smooth twist, pulled them apart.

"What?" I said with my voice filled with unbelief. "How did you do that, Opa?"

"Where you have no one to guide you, you will fail, but with many instructors you will succeed," he said. "Hannah, how are the dolls nesting?"

"I got them all back together, Opa, but my fingers are getting cold too."

Over the past three weeks, taking us into November, the weather had turned decidedly colder. I was glad when Hannah reached into her bag and started handing out the scarves, hats, and mittens she had knitted with the Duchess.

"These are one hundred percent wool," she announced. "The Duchess told me it is the warmest material that can be used for knitting. Sheep can stay outside all winter because of it."

"And we thank you so much, dear Hannah. You have blessed us. Your hard work paid off," encouraged Opa. *"Whoever brings blessing will be blessed, and one who waters will himself be watered."*

The mittens felt wonderful because the back of the truck had no heating and we could see our breath misting around us when Grandfather turned on his magnetic light to check the time. The truck rattled along slowly on a smooth road for almost two hours.

"We should be arriving in Enschede soon," spoke Opa. It didn't surprise me when, at that very moment—as if he could see through the wooden box and walls of the truck—the brakes squealed and we pulled to a stop.

"Now we have a plan to work on," Opa said. "Hannah, here is a pencil and a sharpener. I am not worried about the pencil, but I need a large pile of shavings. Shave them into your mitten so we don't lose any. Hans, this is a box of matches. I need you to take about half of them out and tie them all together with this piece of string." It sounded like just busy work to me, but our grandfather had proved many times over that he knew exactly what he was doing.

"Henry, you need to take the shoelaces out of all of our shoes and tie them together into one piece. Do you remember how to tie those knots we practiced?"

"Of course. I got it."

Opa handed each of us a piece of chewing gum with the instructions to chew on them for a while and hand them back. Eww gross, I thought. We all got to chewing.

Suddenly, the truck pulled to the side of the road and we heard loud angry words yelled from outside. The driver's door slammed, then we heard the back doors of the truck open. Hannah grabbed my arm. Opa gave a quiet "shhh." It must have snowed because footsteps crunched on snowy ground.

An authoritative voice demanded, "What is in this crate?"

We heard Oskar's cheerful reply. "Ahh, I have a piano listed on the shipping manifest, as you can see here, but I am also transporting some escaped spies who have been hiding in Osnabrück."

Did I hear him right? Did he just tell the soldiers that he was transporting spies?

"Don't make jokes, you idiot! That will get you nothing but trouble. Why are you traveling at night? Are you trying to smuggle illegal contraband?"

"Not at all, officer. I am sorry to cause you this inconvenience. This must be a lonely outpost with only two of you posted here. I travel at night because there is less traffic. I know that you are just obeying orders. As am I."

"Never mind. I need to see inside this case. How do I get it open?" asked the angry voice.

"Here, Sergeant. There are convenient latches so you can open and inspect it." We heard the latches open and saw pinholes of light as the soldier shined a flashlight into the case. He grunted as if satisfied.

"See, it is only a piano," said Oskar. "And a very fine one. I have been sent to have it repaired. Can you not contact your headquarters to verify my papers?"

"No. The snow has brought down the phone lines."

"You have a vehicle. I would be glad to follow one of you to the nearest post and ..."

"Shut up, idiot. We only have one vehicle. We are forbidden to leave the post with only one soldier. In any case, you cannot go any farther. The regional Commandant sent word to detain all vehicles. Three spies, two young men and an older one, are attempting to escape. You will wait until the Commandant arrives." The back doors slammed shut again.

"Aha," whispered Opa. "Oskar has done a wonderful job of feeding us information. Only two men on duty, no communication with headquarters, and only one vehicle."

"But Opa," whispered Hans, "we can't just sit here until the Commandant arrives. We will surely be dragged back to Munster and put in jail."

"Or worse, sent to the camps," said Hannah with a shudder.

"Oh no, friends. This is a puzzle, like the nails you were working on, Henry. It seems impossible, but here is our plan ..."

The Gestapo headquarters in Osnabrück was cramped. The Commandant could tell by looking that discipline and diligence had become lax and the soldiers had become lazy. He immediately took command. "Bring me all the travel request papers filled out in the past week." He demanded they be delivered to his desk within the hour. He singled out the only closed-panel truck as suspicious. It had departed from the house of Hildegard von Bismarck, headed north. "Send a squad of soldiers to the Duchess's palace right now to investigate," he roared.

One pair of children's socks found under a bed proved to him that the spies had been there. The Duchess, immediately arrested and brought to headquarters, told them nothing. Orders were issued to capture the truck transporting the piano. Anyone inside must be captured. The Commandant was correct. The leadership had been remiss and the soldiers were slacking. They would pay dearly.

Escape Twelve

"Truth is better than Lies"

The Journal of Henry Gutmann
Rheine, Germany - November 1939

It was tight in the guardhouse with Oskar, two guards, and a potbellied stove which kept it moderately warm, even with the cold night pressing in from outside. A candle replaced the electric light because of fallen power lines.

Inside the truck, Opa and the three young ones could see their breath forming a sheen of ice on the wall of the hidden compartment.

"Are we going to freeze to death?" whispered Hans, worrying about everything.

"Not at all, my friends. It is time now to put our plan into action." He went on to describe a very risky escape that I thought would never work.

As it got later in the guardhouse, the soldiers began to get drowsy.

"I need to relieve myself," said Oskar. "I will return shortly."

"Give me your truck keys," the older soldier said. "We don't want you driving away."

"Of course, Sergeant. I know you don't want me to drive off with those spies in the back of the truck, do you?" He chuckled softly.

"Go, but come back immediately."

"Ya vol, and Heil Hitler," said Oskar as he stepped through the windowless door of the guardhouse, bent over as if to tie his boot lace, and walked away.

With the heater blasting and Oskar laughing like a lunatic, we charged down the snowy road in the truck, all five of us crammed in the front seat to get warm. There had been no heating back in the secret chamber with the piano. It felt wonderful.

"Whoo hoo! That's what to do!" shouted Hans. "You did it again, Opa. How did you get their vehicle to blow up? And Oskar, why did the soldiers not come out and start shooting?"

"Well, trapping the soldiers was the easy part," answered Oskar. "The door had a lock hasp on it that I noticed when we went into the guardhouse. When I stepped out, one of my bootlaces wrapped through the hasp and tied around the handle made it impossible for them to get out. They did yell quite a bit when the truck blew up, and they tried to shoot the handle off the door. I can imagine them screaming with bullets ricocheting around the inside of the guardhouse. It had to be very funny." He laughed again.

"But Opa," asked Hannah, "how *did* you get their truck to blow up? And don't tell us some tall tale."

Opa chuckled with Oskar and told his part of the story.

"I have to tell the truth because, *'Truthful lips endure forever, but a lying tongue is but for a moment.'* So here is what happened when I snuck out of our secret compartment. Crawling on my stomach under our truck, across the road, and under the military vehicle parked by the guardhouse, I got to work. Dragging the bedpan with the pile of projects you had put together, I got into place directly under the fuel tank. I needed my Swiss Army Knife to remove the plug. Every fuel tank has a drain plug, but I had to twist it out, with the bedpan ready to catch the gas pouring out. I plugged the hole with the chewing gum you gave me. I dropped the shoelaces into the bedpan with the gas, holding one end to keep it dry. If you remember my warning, petrol is very flammable and you can't light matches anywhere near it because it will explode.

"Backing up, I pulled the end of the shoelaces with me, making sure the other end stayed in the bedpan." Grandfather told the story with all the mystery of a spy novel. We were sitting with our eyes wide and it occurred to me we had been accused of being spies. That was why they were chasing us. They were convinced of it because of all these clever escapes Opa had engineered, this last one being the most clever yet.

"When I got to the end of the shoelaces, they reached about two meters from the back of the vehicle. Now, I had to move quickly so the laces would not dry out, but if I lit the laces on fire they would burn too fast and set the bedpan on fire before I could get back to our truck. Placing all the pencil shavings in a straight line and lighting them would let it burn slowly and give me the time I needed.

"I looked over and saw Oskar tying the door to the guardhouse and I knew it was time to go. The matches lit right away and I laid them in a pile of shavings, watching to make sure the fire would spread down the line. I knew the shoelaces would burn fast, the gas in the bedpan would catch fire, melt the chewing gum in the plug hole, and eventually, as the gas poured out, the entire truck would explode.

"BOOM!" he shouted. We all jumped.

That is exactly what had happened. Oskar and Opa got to our truck at the same time, started the engine with a spare key hidden beneath the floor mat, and roared off with us bouncing around in the back. Eventually they stopped at a wide part of the road and let us climb in front with them. As we all squeezed in, oh boy, did the warmth feel wonderful.

"What I want to know, Oskar, is why did you tell the soldiers that you were transporting spies?"

"Well, Henry, most of the time, if you are suspected of something, tell people the simple truth. They'll think you are lying. Isn't that the way the Good Book says, Opa?"

"Of course, Oskar. We should always speak the truth if possible. Then we have the Lord's joy. *'Deceit is in the heart of those who devise evil, but those who plan peace have joy.'*"

I guess in some backward way it made sense. If someone is convinced that you are going to lie, even if you tell them the truth they won't believe you. I remembered a time in class when the teacher had called on me to find out why I had not joined the Hitler Youth. I told her I was not interested.

"That is a lie!" she yelled. "Your parents have forbidden you to join, haven't they! They are *refuseniks* and you are a stupid puppet to obey them."

The Hitler Youth was not something I wanted to be a part of. They were the puppets having their strings pulled by Hitler. If I had blamed my parents, they would have gotten in trouble anyway. My parents had always told me to tell the truth.

We were making good time and the signs showed that Rheine was getting closer. The map showed it right across the border in Holland. The closer we got, the farther away it seemed.

As the sun rose, we pulled into the village of Rheine, a lovely town, but I noticed most of the shops had been shuttered with a yellow Star of David painted on the front door. Groups of dejected people clustered on street corners as if they had nothing to do. Soldiers standing around with guns made everyone nervous.

"Are we going to keep going?" asked Hans. "I am getting hungry."

"We have a Jewish friend here in Rheine," said Opa, "Solomon ben Isaac, rabbi of a local synagogue."

"What is a synagogue and a rabbi?" asked Hans. Hannah answered that one.

"A rabbi," she said, as if teaching a class, "is the leader of a synagogue, like the pastor of your church."

"We used to go to a Lutheran church near where we lived in Munster," I added. "They called it Lutheran because it had been started by a man a couple hundred years ago called Martin Luther. They have lots of Lutheran churches all over Germany. Some have been shut down because they refused to follow Hitler's rules and expose the Jews."

Three more turns and we were on a narrow street that wandered into a part of town where there were even more yellow stars. Oskar finally pulled up to a beautiful white building with wooden beams holding up the portico and reaching way up to a white tower with colorful stained-glass windows pointing toward the heavens. On one side of the glass-windowed tower, red paint had been splashed with the words, "Jews go home." Looking over at Hannah, I saw sadness on her face.

"They want us to go home," she said softly, "but we have no home."

"That is true for now," said Opa, "but the Lord says there will be a time when you will have a home. For *'the wicked will be overthrown and will be no more, but the home of the righteous stands forever.'"*

Oskar jumped out of the van and opened the side door for us. "Quickly now, friends, we must get you inside before we are seen." Standing by tall wooden doors, we shivered in the cold dawn light, and I wondered what sort of terrible situation we would find ourselves in next.

A spry, slender man with a leather face, at least a hundred years old, opened the side door of the synagogue and waved us in. He shook hands with Oskar and gave Grandfather an affectionate hug.

"Greetings, my friends." He patted each one of us on the head and said "Y'varechecha Adonai v'yish'm'recha." In German he repeated "May God bless you and keep you."

It warmed my heart that everybody knew and loved my grandfather. Also, it seemed ironic that my parents had been hiding Jews in our home in Munster and now a Jewish rabbi was hiding us in his synagogue.

"Come," he said as he waved us through a heavy wooden door, down a flight of steps, and into a dimly lit basement. "We have a shelter for you." Here was food on a low table and mattresses standing in the corner. "You are welcome to stay as long as you need, friends."

"Oskar," said Grandfather, giving him a concerned look, "will you be secure, my friend? You have done such a heroic task in risking your own life to save ours."

"Ha! It has been an adventure, my friend. I loved doing it." Hans had a sad look on his face. I'm sure he did not think we would ever see Oskar again.

After giving each of us a strong embrace, Oskar left us behind with Rabbi Solomon ben Isaac. I did not know that we would never see Oskar again. I also did not know that Opa would again have to rescue us from being caught by the Nazis.

This time he would use a couple of corks, a bent coat hanger, wet blankets, and a song.

The meal that Rabbi Solomon placed before us was simple but plentiful. It consisted of a pile of unleavened bread, a vegetable paste he called *hummus*, and different kinds of fruit. Bowing our heads while he prayed a blessing over the meal in a sing-song voice, we were reminded that we were filled with gratitude. Hannah, I noticed, had tears in her eyes when she lifted her head. Hans, the first to chow down, also launched into some stories of how Opa had rescued us from our various troubles. I was enthusiastic about the tales Hans spilled out, even if I knew our mother would have reprimanded him for talking with his mouth full. As he started to slow down, the rabbi could see that all our eyes were heavy. We needed rest.

"Come, friends, I know you have had a long night. I have a couple of mattresses to lay on the floor in our storage room. Though not the most comfortable, they will give you a place to sleep." A sparse kitchen and a bathroom with a single light hanging from the ceiling and only cold water coming from the tap gave us a place to clean up. It was a giant step down from the elegant palace where we had been treated like royalty by the Duchess. The storage room had no light at all. Only two mattresses were on the floor, so we lined up. Opa against the wall, Hans next, and Hannah, who seemed to have become quite attached, lay down with me on the outside. Thin blankets we pulled up to our shoulders kept us warm enough, but we were so tired we could have slept on the cement floor with our heads on a rock.

We slept the whole day through. When we groggily started waking up, Opa announced that it was night again.

"We should be able to sneak out tonight and walk to the border. By my calculations, we are only three kilometers away. It is an easy walk. I could probably walk that on my hands."

I knew that, even at his age, Opa could, in fact, still walk on his hands. He had showed us at a picnic in the park in Munster, which seemed like years ago. I laughed at the thought of him walking through the streets of Rheine on his hands.

Suddenly, a crash and the sound of breaking glass startled us. Even in the unlit basement, I knew we were all sitting up.

"What made that noise?" Hannah's voice quavered. Another loud crash, followed by the tinkling sound of falling shards, almost sounding like music, drifted down from above. We could hear voices. Shouting in anger, they became a roar of violence punctuated by more crashes and more broken glass. Hans began sobbing.

"Shh, let us keep silent until we know," came Opa's calm voice from the darkness. I started to crawl my way to the door to find out what was going on, but Hannah's two hands gripped my arm. The door I crawled toward on my hands and knees slid open, revealing Rabbi Solomon with a ghostly white face. Lit by a lone candle, he slipped into the room and closed the heavy metal door behind him. I watched him set the candle on a bench and then lift a sturdy board that dropped into sockets on either side, barricading us in.

"The door is camouflaged on the outside," he said in a voice still gravelly with sleep. "They cannot find us here, but it sounds as if the whole town has turned against us. They are attacking the synagogues and stores." In fact, it did sound like a mob smashing and destroying everything above our heads.

They might not be able to find us, I thought, but we might not get out alive. The crashes continued for what seemed like hours. Fear began to grip me as the smell of smoke drifted through cracks in the ceiling and walls. Heat radiated down and I knew the synagogue was on fire. *We are going to be cooked alive!* I wanted to say, but our incredible grandfather of the optimistic outlook spoke first.

"Aha, I believe they have set the building on fire. We must prepare with what we have. Rabbi, am I correct in assuming that most of the structure is made of stone?"

"Yah, you are correct. The synagogue, built of stone and mortar, will last as long as possible."

"That is good news. It will not completely burn, so we have a healthy chance of surviving. Hans, Henry, take these blankets to the bathroom and soak them with water. Leave the water running since we are also going to drag the mattresses over and soak them too."

In the dim light of the candle, we hurried to do it, dragging and soaking everything we could. Opa pulled a handful of corks from one pocket and plugged the two sink drains in the bathroom and the kitchen. Soon water had filled them and spilled all over the floor. A towel stuffed into the toilet plugged up the sewer and, by lifting the lid off the tank and holding the float arm underwater with a bent coat hanger, water from the bowl spilled out onto the floor.

"Now, we all must lie on the floor beneath the mattresses. Hold the wet blankets over your nose and mouth. You don't want to breathe in any smoke if possible." The heat continued to get more intense and even the water pouring from the sink seemed to get hotter. At one point, Opa soaked another towel. He crawled to the door and touched it to the handle. A violent hiss erupted around the towel, forcing him to drop it and crawl back through the water on the floor. The candle finally guttered and went out.

The night settled into silence.

In the darkness, we heard the deep voice of Opa as he began to sing. *"Deceit is in the hearts of those who plan evil, but joy is for those who make peace. Harm will not overtake the righteous, but for the wicked trouble will never cease."* It was a simple melody, so by the third time he sang it, we were all singing softly along with him. *"Deceit is in the hearts of those who plan evil, but joy is for those who make peace. No harm will overtake the righteous, but for the wicked trouble will never cease."*

Even lying in a puddle under a soggy mattress, I closed my weary eyes, hoping to drift off to sleep. I could hear Hans begin to breathe heavily and even Hannah twitched as she slept next to me. I could not.

Thinking back about this whole adventure, as I wrote it down, I was convinced that no one would believe Opa was going to be able to rescue us again. This time with a pile of broken glass, two car hubcaps, a birdfeeder pole, and burning rags.

After a while, I finally slipped off to sleep.

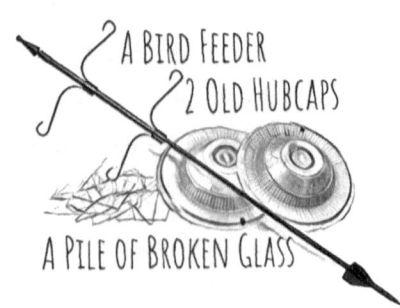

A BIRD FEEDER

2 OLD HUBCAPS

A PILE OF BROKEN GLASS

Scraping from the heavy metal door woke me. Grandfather and Rabbi Solomon were trying to pull it open.

⋮

Smoke still rose from the burned-out military vehicle outside the roadside checkpoint. Two soldiers, shivering in the cold light of morning, watched the Commandant fume and bellow in their faces.

"You imbeciles! You idiots! You incompetents! How could two children and a doddering old man lock you in the guardhouse, set your truck on fire, and escape into the night!? Well ... answer me!"

"Th-there was no old man. We saw no children. The driver had a trained group of commandos who locked us in the booth and set our truck on fire. They were highly trained at military sabotage. We didn't have a chance."

"Liars!" the Commandant screamed with spittle running down his chin. "Liars! And lying will only get you both shot. It was children and an old man who tricked you and locked you into the booth. You will pay for this."

Escape Thirteen

"LIGHT IS BETTER THAN DARKNESS"

The Journal of Henry Gutmann
Rheine, Germany - November 1939

Grey light filtered through the opening as I struggled to help Grandfather and Rabbi Solomon push and pull charred timbers out of the way so we could escape from the chamber where we almost cooked like roast chickens. When all five of us managed to climb up the burned stairway, it was heartbreaking to see the lovely synagogue in ruins. We walked, crunching broken glass under our feet, out into the street, where every storefront window had been smashed and most of the buildings were burned. Smoke still rose from piles of rubble. Not a single person could be seen outdoors.

"I predict that this night will go down in history," choked Rabbi Solomon ben Isaac with tears in his eyes. "It will be forever known as *Kristallnact*—The Night of Broken Glass."

As he spoke, the sun's rays coming over the ruined buildings shone on the carpet of broken glass, turning the devastation into a field of glistening diamonds.

Opa walked out into the middle of the street, looked around, and spoke as if from deep sorrow. "*'We will be rewarded as we say good things, even when faithless people only want violence.'* I pray Oskar made it across the border yesterday." Turning back to us, he continued, "Well, Rabbi, I'm grieved that your lovely synagogue is destroyed and I pray that none of your people were hurt. Surely they knew this might come and hid themselves."

"We've seen it coming for years." Rabbi Solomon nodded, his grey head covered with soot. "The time of Jacob's trouble is now upon us."

"Perhaps if it is, dear friend, the time of your redemption is near and your land will be returned to your people. *A longing fulfilled will be light and sweetness to your soul.*'"

"Opa," asked Hannah, "are you saying that my people will have a land we can return to?"

"That is exactly what I am saying, Hannah. The rabbi and I have discussed this often." He chuckled and turned a weary smile toward his friend. "We agree that you will have a land to call your own, but," he went on, "who will provide it, and when, is still under discussion."

"Yah, and your depth of understanding of our own writings always amazes me, you old Gentile. I pray that we will talk again. Now you must go. You will have to go on foot because nothing but tanks with metal tires could drive on this glass." He handed a meager bag of leftover food to Hannah, pushing all of us to move on. "At the top of the hill, ask at the white house on the corner for Zigfried. He can lead you to a safe place and a path to the border. Now, go quickly." Rabbi urged.

Trudging uphill on the road out of town was weary work, but Opa still seemed light of step and even began whistling the song we sang last night in the basement.

"Opa," said Hannah, shaking her head, "why do people burn and destroy things? It makes me so sad."

"That is a simple question to answer, Hannah. People can be stirred up by evil leaders. They are told they deserve what others have. When they see others doing well, they are told to be angry and jealous. They are incited to destroy even what others have built.

"Solomon, a wise man, worked hard and built stables, houses, roads, and palaces, but his sons wanted to have it all without the work. Solomon even wrote that *'If you work hard you will be rewarded'* and *'If you get things by cheating it will all disappear. But those who build a little at a time will prosper.'"*

We walked along in silence, but I could tell Hannah was thinking hard. Her nose crinkled up and her eyebrows scrunched together. She looked cute like that.

When she finally spoke, she seemed almost angry. "What happened to Solomon's sons?" she asked. "Were they bad?"

"That is a sad part of history. When parents are not faithful in teaching their young ones from God's wisdom, everything begins falling apart in the next generation. Did your parents ever try to teach you something you didn't want to learn?"

Her face changed and she laughed. I liked that.

"Oh yes, my mother made sure I knew the difference between right and wrong."

"Did she ever discipline you for doing wrong?" Opa asked gently.

"She never disciplined me for the first time, or if it was an accident. If it was intentional or I was trying to get away with something or being dishonest, I would really get it." She laughed and I laughed with her. She rolled her eyes.

"Mama never disciplined me when she was angry or frustrated. She would wait until she calmed down and very quietly say, 'Hannah dear, bring me the switch.'"

"Yikes! Hide in a ditch," said Hans. "Mama has grabbed the switch!" We all laughed, knowing exactly what that was about.

"Oh yes," said Opa. "The wisdom in The Book says it well. *'Parents who do not discipline must hate their children, but if they love them they are careful to teach them at all times.'"*

I looked over at Hannah, but the laughter had gone from her face. I knew she was thinking about her parents and how they had been taken to the concentration camp. What a horrible thought. Trying to get her mind off that, I picked up a piece of the broken glass on the street and showed her how the sunlight sparkled off it.

Opa noticed what I was doing and commented. "Do you see how the light changes colors? That is how we get a rainbow in the sky when the sunlight reflects through the raindrops. The rainbow is a reminder that the earth will never be flooded like in the days of Noah. We are even told that we can become rainbows as we reflect the light of God. *'The lives of good people are a light that shines more brightly every day.'"*

I could see in Hannah's eyes that her thoughts were still on finding a way to return to be with her parents. It weighed heavy on me, knowing that Hans and I wanted the same thing.

We rested in the back seat of a burned-out car and ate some of the meager food the rabbi had provided. The water had all been drunk. I worried that we would get thirsty soon. Nobody talked as we ate, but Grandfather finished eating quickly and began scavenging around in the rubble of some burned-out buildings. When he returned, he carried a sack filled with strange lumpy shapes and a tall birdfeeder pole he was using as a walking stick. He also had a large jug of water.

"Opa," Hannah gushed. "You can find anything." I noticed the bag with the lumpy contents and knew he had some sort of a plan.

"Come, team, we must keep moving. Remember, *'Sound judgment is praised, but people without good sense are on their way to disaster.'"* The uphill climb started to level off, showing us the view of the valley below. By this time the sun began to set low in the sky behind us. Shadows were long in front of us, sloping down onto the plain below.

Hope and fear crashed in at the same time. Hope, because the road ran almost straight downhill and we could actually see the Holland border. Fear, because between us and the border were hundreds, maybe thousands of tanks, armored vehicles, and troops spread out before us. Filling every roadway, blocking every crossing, parked in every driveway, even parking lots at stores and shops were crammed with the military machines of the Führer. We were doomed if they spotted us and started up the road in our direction.

"Okay, dear ones, it is time for a new plan," said Opa calmly. Turning to me, he handed over the Swiss Army Knife he always carried.

"See that wrecked car alongside the road? Pry two of the hubcaps off and bring them here. We must distract the tanks and get them to veer off the road at this point."

"Hannah," he said as he pulled a pair of work gloves out of one of his pockets, "put these on so you don't cut yourself, and collect a number of shards of the thickest glass you can find and put them in the bag. Hans, I need you to find a square stone we can use as a hammer, and some rags."

Walking quickly up a narrow side street, we finally stopped at a high point between two stone houses. Opa took the birdfeeder pole and began driving it into the ground until he had hammered it down to as high as Hannah's head. Piercing the two hubcaps with the Swiss Army Knife, he threaded the first down the pole until it stopped at the birdfeeder hook. Reaching into his bag, he pulled out a hose clamp and a ball bearing. The hose clamp got tightened right above the first hubcap, with the ball bearing above it.

This seemed to be the strangest contraption I had seen Grandfather build yet. He took the second hubcap and cut angled slots in it all the way around so it looked like a fan blade.

The second hubcap settled on the pole and he slowly filled it with the broken glass, using the gloves and carefully moving the shards around till they were perfectly balanced.

"Now the rags, Hans." Placing them in the lower hubcap, Opa pulled a can of oil from his sack and poured some onto the rags.

"Wave the flags and burn the rags," said Hans after he placed them in the hubcap .

"Flint and steel now, Henry. You have had some practice using them. Light it up!" On the second strike, the rags burst into flames and the heat began to rise. I don't know how Opa had managed to craft those pieces of junk so cleverly, but the upper hubcap began to spin.

A memory popped into my head of a wooden merry-go-round lamp in my bedroom with tiny horses on it that would slowly begin to spin when the light was turned on. Opa had explained how heat from the bulb would create warm air, making it rise, spinning the fan and causing the horses to go around and around. Watching the silent motion eventually would put me to sleep.

On Opa's contraption, light from the flames shone through the slots, reflected off the glass, and began shooting around us like a military signal light. As darkness descended, the flashing light looked like a semaphore, sending signals across the valley, where the tanks were certain to see them.

"But Opa," said Hannah, getting nervous again, "do we want the tanks to find us?"

"Not at all, child. This light is intended to lure them up here while we go down there. Now we must find our guide, for *'One who gives wise instruction is like a life-giving fountain, and they will help us to escape all deadly traps.'"*

Opa looked up at the house beside us and breathed a long whistle. A fearful face appeared in a second-story window.

"Hello, friend!" shouted Opa. "You are Zigfried? Come down quickly. You must broadcast some news."

In moments, a young man wearing the traditional Jewish beanie, or *yarmulke* as Hannah had told me to call it, appeared beside us.

"What's your name, son?"

"I'm Zigfried, but my friends call me Zig."

"Very well, to us you are Zig. Do you know of any secret paths to the border?"

He nodded nervously.

"Good. First you must go warn your friends that the Nazi tanks will be coming up the road soon. They will think your people are sending out signals for help. They must hide if they can. Remember *'a trustworthy messenger brings words of safety.'* You must meet us on the main road and lead us along those hidden paths to the border."

Our new friend rushed off as we headed back toward the road. In moments, Zig returned with a lamp, ready to guide us on our way.

"We can make it down the path until they cannot find us. There, for a time, you must hide," he told us. "Come quickly. My aunt has a house halfway to the border."

You cannot even believe that bales of hay, three horse blankets, six horseshoes, a spool of black thread, and a blacksmith's hammer made up the interesting collection of items Opa used

in rescuing us again from the Nazis. I promise I am not making this up.

⋮

"We will catch them," the Commandant muttered through clenched teeth. With the two sentries fading into the rearview mirror, the convoy roared on toward Rheine. His instructions to the command post there had been clear. "Stir up the mob against the Jews." If they are hiding the old man, they will pay. "Send rioters to start fires, burn their books, their homes. Destroy businesses and synagogues," he told them. He would show this band of troublemakers who had the power, and he would smash them with a mighty fist. Soon this ridiculous chase would be over. He knew how to wield the rod of authority, and it would destroy this town and crash down upon the heads of these inferior and dangerous people. After all, he was the Commandant.

Escape Fourteen

"PRUDENT IS BETTER THAN PROUD"

The Journal of Henry Gutmann
On foot at the crossroads, Germany - November 1939

Opa's makeshift signal light was still flashing light down into the dark valley, beaming brighter as night fell. We knew the soldiers saw it. Headlights from a handful of military vehicles turned toward us, pointing uphill, piercing the dark much brighter than Opa's semaphore.

"Now we must be prudent, friends," Opa admonished seriously.

"What does that mean, Opa?" Hannah asked.

"Ah, that is so important, Hannah. Being prudent is making wise plans. *'Silly people will believe anything, but the prudent give careful thought to their steps.'"*

"That sounds smart. Do you have a plan, Opa?" Hannah asked.

Hans didn't give him a chance to answer. Pointing at the headlights climbing the hill, he said fearfully, "I feel like a frog, Opa. Do you remember when you took us frog hunting at night?"

"Of course, Hans, we carried flashlights, looking for two tiny red eyes, and tried to scoop them up in our nets."

"Did you catch them?" asked Hannah.

"Oh yeah," answered Hans. "They were huge, and we caught buckets full."

"What did you do with buckets of giant frogs?"

"We ate them." I laughed. "They were delicious."

"Frogs?! Yuck," said Hannah, pointing her finger down her throat. "What did they taste like?"

"They tasted like chicken," I said.

"You say everything tastes like chicken," said Hans.

"Well, you did scoop them up like you were starving."

"I hope the Nazis don't scoop us up with a big swoop." Hans shivered.

"Children, we are not frogs, and we know that eventually the enemy will fail. *'The house of the wicked will be destroyed, but the tent of the upright will flourish.'*"

"Come, we must go before they arrive," whispered our guide. "The road winds, but they are driving fast."

In the gloom ahead, army tanks speared their headlights up the hill toward us. What we didn't know was that the Commandant and his henchmen were pulling into Rheine just minutes behind us.

Broken glass no longer under our feet, the valley below was now as black as the lake where we caught frogs. Ahead, pinpoint lights were scattered around the dark valley like frogs' eyes, but I could tell where the border was, because beyond that line there were no lights at all.

"Opa," I whispered back, "why are there no lights on the other side of the border?"

"It is because of the night bombing runs the Nazis have begun in Holland. They are even targeting hospitals and schools. It is a cruel tactic."

We stumbled often, trying to follow the dim lamp. Hannah clutched my hand, Hans bumped into us once in a while, and Opa brought up the rear. Soon we were leaving the village. The trail became steeper as we descended into the valley. Our guide knew the way and had the lamp, so he regularly had to slow down, turning to wait on our faltering progress. I worried about my grandfather, who was beginning to breathe a bit heavier and lagged farther behind. A few quick steps brought me up beside Zigfried. My hand clutched his shoulder as I whispered, "We must rest for a moment."

Over a rise to our right, a hill blocked the view of the military vehicles and tanks, but we could hear them roaring up the road toward us. As we paused for breath, we could even hear the angry shouts of Nazi soldiers on the road beyond. Between the noise and shouts, Opa murmured softly, *"Fools are hotheaded, and quick-tempered people do really foolish things."*

It was fully night. We could not tell how far we had come, but we could feel the path turning into the hills and moving away from the town and the main road. We walked quietly for a time. Abruptly, a white house came into view with a dim light shining through the cracks in the shutters and under the door. Zig whistled the same notes Opa had and the door swung open as if we were expected.

A pleasant-faced woman welcomed us in.

"Please come in, weary travelers. I am Anna, Zig's aunt. Welcome. News of your adventures has reached us through those you have met along the way. We have laughed about how you fooled the Commandant over and over again." Humbly, she bowed and ushered us into her warm home and began pulling food out of her pantry.

News traveled through some kind of secret network, and many people were willing and able to help us on our journey.

"Thank you most kindly," replied Opa with a bow. "We know that *A wise woman builds her house … She fears the Lord and walks in a prudent way.'"*

Zig helped bring food to the wooden table with four chairs where we sat. Opa bowed his head and prayed for protection on this house, the generous people who shared it, and safety for our journey. Trying not to look as starved as we were, we started shoving food into our mouths.

"Did you really leave a German soldier beside the road with no clothes on?" Zig asked as he brought more food.

"Well …" said Hannah with a giggle, "we did leave his underwear on."

Of course, Hans had to put his spin on it.

"Yes sir, Zig, that Nazi was really rude and we left him almost nude."

Our kind hostess laughed out loud. "In these dark times it is healthy to laugh, even if it is only for a brief time."

"So true," murmured Opa after swallowing. *"Laughter is as good as medicine … even if your heart aches while you laugh and rejoicing ends in grief.*" I know where he quoted from, but he said it with a note of sorrow in his voice, well aware that thousands of hearts were aching.

"Well, I hope you have eaten your fill," said Anna, even though Hans still tried to fit one last piece of chicken into his mouth. "My house is inadequate to have you sleep in here, but the barn out back where we used to keep our oxen for plowing and horses for riding is empty and has sweet hay and blankets."

"Not to worry, my lady. *'Your strong ox no doubt gave you abundant harvest, but where there is no ox the manger is clean,'*" assured Opa.

"What does that mean, Opa?" asked Hannah.

"No mystery there," I answered. "When you have an ox, it plows your fields and you can grow plenty of food, but an ox will make a mess in the barn."

"Yeah," said Hans, holding his nose, "no ox, no manure, no mess to endure."

"Oh hush," replied Hannah, punching him in the arm. "I get it."

He kept on and said, "No stink, I think."

I shook my head as we were led by Zig and his lamp from the warm house into the darkness. We all thanked Anna and hugged her on the way out. The barn had been kept clean and empty except for a criss-cross stack of hay bales.

"Hmmm," Opa grunted, looking around the barn. I began to imagine what was going on in his head. He was trying to figure out how we could be hidden from the soldiers. "Zig, is there no basement or attic where we can hide in case the soldiers show up?"

"No, I am so sorry. This is all we have." He shrugged his shoulders.

"It will do, but I think we should have a plan, just in case."

Rummaging around, he flipped open two blankets and found a collection of metal horseshoes and a worn hammer.

"Your father worked as a blacksmith?"

"Yes," Zig said as he looked away. "Before the Nazis took him away. He was a good father and a good man."

"Take heart, young Zig. *'Eventually the faithless will be fully repaid for their evil ways and the good rewarded.'*"

Putting prudence into practice, Opa instructed me to climb up to the pole rafters with the two blankets and drape them from one to the next. The horseshoes were exactly the right size to fit over the poles, which we hammered down to create four hammocks. *How did Opa figure that out?*

"Friends, we have comfortable places to sleep, with hopes that the soldiers will not look up. We do need some kind of alarm. Hans, you tie the leftover horseshoe to the end of this thread and we will hang it over the hammock. Henry, I will toss the spool over the beam and you thread it through that crack in the wall. String it about ankle-high all the way across the pathway, as far as it will reach, and tie it well, down low on the base of a tree."

"What is Opa doing now, Henry?" asked Hannah as she followed me down to the trail.

"Opa wants me to set up a trip wire with the thread. If the soldiers come up the path they will break the thread, which will drop the horseshoe onto our hammock."

"Please don't hang it where it might land on my head." She giggled. I was glad that she seemed in better spirits.

"I like to hear you laugh, Hannah. One of Opa's favorite quotes is *'A happy heart makes a cheerful face.'*" With the trip wire in place, we headed back to the barn.

"All done, Opa," I said as I handed him the spool of thread.

"Wonderful, Henry. This thread is thin enough that they will never feel it against their boots when it breaks. But it will drop the horseshoe onto our hammock."

Thinking of what Hannah had said made me laugh. "Opa, Hannah wants you to make sure it is not hanging over her head." He got a grin on his face, put a finger to his lips, and winked at Hannah.

"I think we should hang it over Hans's hammock." Turning, he said, "Zig, if you will scatter the hay bales around the barn after we climb up, we should be set for the night."

Climbing up the hay bales and stretching out in our horse blanket hammocks did not take long. We were tired. Sleep would come quickly. Before we nodded off, I whispered over to My grandfather.

"Opa, how did you know how to find all these kind people to help us on our journey?"

His voice already heavy with oncoming sleep, he answered, *"You know those who plot evil will go astray, but those who plan what is good find love and faithfulness."*

Hannah and Hans were sound asleep, but my eyes were wide open, staring into the backness of the barn. Thoughts and memories of our escapes rolled around in my head and kept me from dozing off. The journey had been hard on Opa. His walk had slowed and more than once he had seemed to be limping as he struggled to keep up. *What would happen if he could not go on? If we were captured, would they take him and leave us kids on our own? Could the three of us keep going? Could we even survive?*

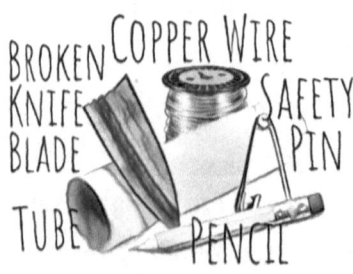

Finally, sleep started to drop down on me like a blanket. Looking back at the beginning of this ordeal, I remembered thinking we would not survive, but we had, with no inkling that our next escape would involve a cardboard tube, a length of copper wire, a lead pencil, a safety pin, and a broken knife blade. It turned out to be an incredible adventure and one I don't think I could ever do again.

Then the horseshoe fell.

The Commandant was now in serious trouble. News of his failures to capture the "spies" had reached the general of the 3rd Panzer Division on the Dutch border. The General and the Commandant met on the main road in Rheine. A giant military tank stopped nose-to-nose with the Commandant's car. The two men got out and faced each other. Ironically, right beside them a strange contraption still containing a flickering flame spun slowly. It had developed a squeak. It was obnoxious in the quiet that descended when the vehicles shut down their engines.

"You, Commandant, have failed! You had a dangerous spy in your grasp and he escaped!" challenged the General, who claimed the higher rank. "You will pay for your failures."

Escape Fifteen

"HONOR IS BETTER THAN FAME"

The Journal of Henry Gutmann
The Dutch border, Enschede, Holland - November 1939

The horseshoe landed on my chest. Instantly wide awake, I reached out to alert the others and, with a quiet hiss, urged silence. Voices of soldiers, a command, and the barn door crashed open. Lights blazed in. It was still dark outside, but the flashlights lit up the inside of the barn.

"They must be hiding somewhere!" shouted the General. "Find them!"

We all lay in our blanket hammocks, as silent as we could. The soldiers swarmed in, shining lights in every corner … but they did not look up. Again, Opa's wisdom astounded me with the decision to hide us in plain sight. From below, the blankets must have looked like a draped cloth ceiling, perhaps to keep some warmth in during the cold winters. It was clearly not obvious that three kids and their grandfather were lying in them. Further shouts out in the yard and the words of our friend Zig, pleading ignorance, hurled through the door.

"Officer, there is no one in the house save my elderly mother and myself. We have been sleeping all night. We have neither seen nor heard any spies." As I heard him say that, I recalled the admonition Opa gave us days ago to tell the truth as much as we are able. It was true. We were not spies and we were not in the house. I prayed for the safety of Anna and Zig. The noise finally subsided. Through the open barn door, we heard the heavy boots march away into the dawn light. We continued to lie perfectly still until a shuffle of feet and the smell of fresh coffee wafted up to the rafters.

"They are gone now," said Zig. "I will stack some hay bales so you can all climb down." And there he stood, like a cheerful cherub, carrying a basket of baked muffins and a tray with coffee. Opa swung over the edge, hung by his hands, and dropped to the floor.

"Light in a messenger's eyes brings joy to the heart," he quoted as he brushed himself off, *"and good news gives health to the bones."*

"All I hear from my bones is moans," spouted our poet.

Helping Zig took only a few moments, stacking the bales in the corner, which allowed us to climb down. I helped Hannah and we sat on the bales as we ate the sweet muffins, peeled oranges, and drank the bittersweet coffee with cream. I think we all slept well, despite Hans's complaints and the early wakeup call, but the thought of having to figure out how to avoid the military buildup at the border and sneak across did not sound fun.

Opa, as jovial as ever, was drawing on the floor of the barn with a stick, getting Zig to help him understand the terrain and how we might get past the massive Nazi army on the Dutch border.

Running footsteps outside the barn surprised us and we all tried to jump behind bales of hay to hide. Zig, walking to the door casually, started to swing it shut.

"Quick, you must hide me," panted a dirty German soldier, pushing past him into the barn. Hair matted with leaves, he was wearing a panicked look on his face and a uniform that had been stripped of all badges and insignias. I recognized him immediately as the German commandant we had first seen on the sidewalk outside the bookstore in Munster. He undoubtedly was our nemesis, the one who had been chasing us for months.

Grandfather stood, nodding sagely. "And why, must I ask, are you seeking asylum?"

"The General has singled me out for punishment, possibly death by firing squad, because of a personal vendetta and blaming me for not capturing an old man and three children." I stood beside Grandfather. Henry and Hannah also stood up. Suddenly his eyes widened and his mouth dropped open.

"You! You are the spy that has made such a fool of me! Because of you I have been stripped of all rank and official status and am now an escaped convict running for my life." He gasped as he ran out of breath. With an angry burst, he cried, "I could kill you!" He lunged toward Grandfather, but Zig held him back. "I tell you, now is the time for reckoning. You four have caused me more trouble than you can possibly imagine, and now you are going to pay. You are going to pay dearly!"

"Here, friend, some of this coffee is still hot," spoke Opa, "and there are," he said as he glanced at me, "five, no, only four, muffins left in the basket for you." He smiled, offering the Commandant the basket.

Tension ran through the Commandant's dirty red face. Zig's restraining hand gripped his arm.

In a quiet little-girl voice, Hannah asked, "Opa, why are you so nice to a man who is so mean?"

With a soft chuckle he answered. "Ah, Hannah, if people only believed the Good Book there would be fewer wars. It says clearly that *A gentle answer turns away wrath, but a harsh word stirs up anger*' and '*A soothing tongue is a tree of life.*'"

"We had heard," said Zig, "of your cleverness and your adventures, Opa, but it has also become known about your wisdom and knowledge of the words of God."

"Yeah," blurted out Hans proudly. "Opa knows every one of Solomon's words ... by heart."

The Commandant eased the tug Zig had on his arm and looked down at the floor. He shook his head. "My mother, God rest her soul, had many of the words of Scripture memorized."

"I am sorry she died," said Opa sadly. "I lost my mother when still a boy. It was very hard for me. When did your mother pass on?"

The anger that had forced him into the barn and had turned on Grandfather seemed to be leaking out like air from a punctured tire. With his eyes still on the floor, he slumped onto one of the bales of hay. "She fought a severe battle with illness and went on just one month ago. She lived a good life, a wise woman who was always happy."

"No doubt that she knew the words," Opa went on, "because *'a happy heart makes a cheerful face,'* and *'a cheerful heart has a continual feast.'*"

Not knowing how to respond, the Commandant reached out for the cup of hot coffee that Opa had been holding. He took the basket also and set it on the floor at his feet. He began to eat the muffins and take sips of coffee. He looked dejected but, since he was still a German soldier, I felt nervous having him sit and eat with us. Hans, on the other hand, who continually amazed me with his pluck, didn't waste any time in speaking up.

"So, Mr. Gestapo man, what did the General accuse you of and how did you escape, huh?"

Anger flamed in the Commandant's eyes, but he was in the minority. He had no weapons, no platoon to command, and his own people were chasing him.

"The General hates me. He accused me of treason. In the Gestapo the penalty for treason is death. He said I actually helped you escape, which would be helping the enemy. I was arrested and placed with two men to escort me to the prison camp at Linden. I escaped." He shrugged his shoulders as if it was an easy thing to do.

"Wow," answered Hans. "We have been trying to escape from the Gestapo. Trust me, I know it ain't easy. But we have a secret weapon. His name is Opa. He is smarter than you and all your Gestapo."

'That kid is going to get us in trouble,' I thought.

But humility was written on Hans's face. The Commandant, head down, focused on the muffins and coffee and did not respond. After a while, he looked over at Grandfather and, with more than grudging respect, asked, "I have seen some of your clever booby traps. How did you learn to do all that?"

"My grandfather knows everything," Hans blurted out as he reached for the last muffin in the basket. "He made a whole zoo of animals folded out of paper someone threw in the trash. You remember that, don't you Opa?"

Opa laughed, which lifted my heart. Even after all the pressure we had been under, his contagious chuckle wrinkled his face into a happy smile. But I knew we were still too far from the safety of Holland, if we could even find safety there.

"The truth is, I have worked a wide variety of different jobs over the years but, very early on, my godly mother began teaching me from the Scriptures. The most valuable things I learned there."

Hans jumped in again, causing me to roll my eyes. "Yeah, he even knows how to get gas out of the tank on a truck."

"I did wonder how he did that. I do remember some of what my mother taught me from the Scriptures, but not much. I stopped going to church when I was still a boy."

"Ahh," said Opa, closing his eyes and putting his head back. "That is the most valuable time to learn these truths which apply to everyone, everywhere." I could tell his mind was tracing back to his childhood years as his voice lifted into a more youthful tone. *"Proverbs teach you wisdom and instruct you.*

They help you understand wise sayings. They provide you with instruction and help you live wisely. They lead to what is right and honest and fair. They give understanding to ignorant people. They give knowledge and good sense to those who are young."

"Well, it is clear that those words helped you on your way. I want to know how you got out the window and crossed the roof in Osnabrück. One of my soldiers tried it and fell thirty feet. Good thing he landed on a brush pile or he would have been killed on the pavement stones."

Hannah, sitting wide-eyed, spoke up. "Grandfather showed us how to be lizards and we crawled across the roof like geckos." Hans did his lizard impersonation and everybody laughed.

A narration of our adventures followed, with Hannah and Hans chiming in with highlights, including Hans quoting poetry and doing his pantomimes. Hannah told about the kind rabbi who protected us during the fire. The question eventually came up about how the Commandant intended to escape from his own men.

Zig left and came back with food for lunch, telling us that from his rooftop he could see the tanks and trucks filling the valley below. "We will have to wait until night falls to try again for the border, but while we wait, eat, rest, and preserve your strength."

Asking questions about the Commandant's childhood in Munich helped me understand more about him. I could hear sadness in his voice when he told us how every young man, at eighteen, was forced into the military. How he became arrogant and proud of his position in the Gestapo. It put a wedge between him and his mother. A family feud started the tension with the General, who became a bitter enemy. Nevertheless, the Commandant worked hard and rose in the ranks all the way to being head of the Gestapo in Munster, eventually being given the job of capturing spies.

"Well, that was a waste," he said bitterly. "All because they told me you were a band of evil saboteurs."

"Did they really tell you that?" I asked, looking him directly in the eyes.

"Yes. Written in the official document I received from the General. I think he made it up and convinced his superiors you are all terrorists! Look at you. A worn-out old man and three children. And I let you escape! Now I am going to die because of it."

"Hey! Don't say that," yelped Hans. "Grandfather is not a worn-out old man and we are not children!"

"What you must bring back to your mind, friend, is what your mother taught you," reminded Opa, "that *'Wisdom will teach you to fear the Lord, and humility comes before honor.'*"

I could tell that the Commandant had become demoralized and wanted no part of the chase.

The day wore on. We lounged on piles of hay while Opa and the Commandant murmured together about their childhood, the coming war and the probable invasion of Holland.

Darkness began reaching into the valley as the sun set beyond Rheine, pointing toward the border and freedom. As night fell, we set out following Zig's bobbing flashlight, which gradually dimmed until right before dawn when the batteries died completely. The Commandant had become part of our group. He even carried Hannah across a creek and some rough terrain, almost as an apology for chasing us across Germany. Hans kept quiet, under penalty of having his mouth taped shut. Opa, stopping often for a breather, brought up the rear. Crossing the valley, with the full military machine off to our right, the path began to rise toward the Dutch-built dikes that marked the border around Holland, where we were headed.

"The path of life leads upward for the prudent," wheezed Opa, slightly out of breath. *"To keep them from going down to the place of the dead."*

Made perfect sense to me. I didn't want any part of that place. Just then a string of barbed wire appeared. It stretched both ways along the dike that blocked our path.

We had reached the border.

Suddenly it all came crashing in on us. My heart sank in my chest. Giant lights smashed through the brush in a roar of dust and exhaust. Soldiers brandishing guns leapt off each side, all weapons pointed right at us. A second military vehicle exploded into the clearing. More soldiers shoved their massive guns in our direction. Everyone seemed to be shouting. Holding Hannah's hand made it easy to pull her behind me. Hans jumped over and grabbed my arm. I jerked my head to the west where I saw the Commandant scramble over the barbed wire, his shadowy bulk disappearing down the other side into Holland.

My real concern was Grandfather. His protective form in front of us was silhouetted in the light of the rising sun. His heavy coat extended like hovering wings as he stood straight and tall. To my eyes, he didn't even look afraid, although I'm sure he was.

We were pinned against the dike, like the frogs in our pond, by the massive headlights from the tanks. Climbing out of the lead tank rose the General.

"Officer," spoke Grandfather, loud with a confidence I could not fathom, "what are you afraid of from these children? They have done no harm."

"Spies! Enemies of the state! You, old man, you will be interrogated and shot. The children will be sent to the prison camps." As two soldiers stepped forward to grab Opa, he backed away and turned toward us.

Facing Hans first, from an upper pocket he pulled that slender book I had seen him read often and handed it to him, saying, "In here you will find *the joy in giving the right answer and know how to give it at the right time!*"

Reaching out like the magician he had always been, the Russian dolls appeared and went to Hannah, saying, "Inside the words you will find safety if you pray, *'The Lord hears the prayers of the righteous.'*" He smiled at me. "Henry, you must wear the mantle for a time. Remember, *'Don't let heaviness crush your spirit, a happy heart will always give you a cheerful face.'* Rescue everyone you can."

Shrugging out of his coat, he handed it to me, along with the responsibility that weighed heavy on my shoulders.

Ready and resigned, Opa faced the soldiers. He patted one on the shoulder as they grabbed him roughly, marching him toward the military vehicles. I saw him stumble, going down on one knee. Hans started forward, calling out, "Opa!" but I grabbed his arm.

Another group of soldiers approached to drag us to the transport. Tear-filled eyes blurred my last view of Opa. Yet, I could still see his cheerful smile as he shouted, "Don't forget, *'The fear of the Lord is a secure fortress, and a safe refuge for the young.'*"

As the soldiers moved closer, a whistle behind me made me turn. With a hoarse whisper, the Commandant revealed himself, poking out from behind a leafy bush.

"Quick! Come, children. You can still escape. The soldiers will not follow you here." Reaching to one side, he lifted the barbed wire to allow us to slip into Holland and freedom.

I hesitated. Glancing back, I saw Opa in the distance between two soldiers. Hans was still taking steps to follow him, and Hannah's tear-stained face turned toward Germany where her parents remained captive. Then, in fear, they both looked back at me.

Opa's coat didn't fit. Well, almost. I had grown enough so that it didn't reach the ground, but the shoulders drooped. The cuffs had to be folded twice so my hands could stick out. I guess it was mine now. Opa's smell hung over the coat, as well as a strong spirit that anything was possible. It felt natural for my hands to slip into the side pockets. The journal I had carried with me to record these stories fit in the left pocket. I hoped

SWISS ARMY KNIFE

there would be more to write. In the other pocket, my right hand felt a clutter of items that I withdrew. Glancing down, the handful revealed a cardboard tube, a length of copper wire, a lead pencil, a safety pin, and a broken knife blade.

Opa was gone. We had no idea where our parents were. All we had left was each other and an old coat with many pockets. And yet, I believed that somehow Opa's legacy would rescue us again.

I heard the insistent hiss. "Come. Quickly! They are not watching."

"No, we cannot." I spoke clearly to the Commandant. "You can escape, but we have to return and rescue anyone we can."

From a low rise on the far side of the border, the Commandant could see us being forced into the military vehicle that was to transport us to the death camps. For the first time since his childhood, he humbly bowed his head and prayed.

"Father, forgive me for my many crimes. I pray for those good people. That old man was humble and wise. His children were kind. 'If I take your correction to heart, I will gain understanding, and wisdom will teach me to fear you, Lord. Now I know that humility comes before honor.' I would also ask, Lord, that you rescue that wise man and his children because of your mercy."

The End of the Journal but not the Story ...

Appendix to Quotations:

Escape One

(pages 11-16)

Proverbs 1:18 - *Evil people hide, but they ambush only themselves!*

Proverbs 21:22 - *A wise person can take on armed soldiers and their weapons will fall.*

Proverbs 1:26 - *He will laugh when disaster strikes them and make fun when calamity overtakes them.*

Proverbs 24:5–6 – *It is better to be wise than strong. Smarts win out over muscle every time.*

Proverbs 1:33 - *Whoever listens to wisdom will live in safety and be at ease, without fear of harm.*

Escape Two

(pages 17-26)

Proverbs 1:15, 16 - *Do not join with them, don't even walk with them; for their feet rush into evil, they are quick to shed blood.*

Proverbs 10:28 - *For the hope of the righteous brings joy.*

Proverbs 15:24 - *The path of life leads upward for the wise; they leave the grave behind.*

Proverbs 2:7 - *He gives good judgment to those who live right.*

Proverbs 24:11, 12 - *So let the wise listen and add to their learning.*

Proverbs 24:11, 12 - *Rescue those who are being dragged off to die; save them as they stagger to their death … "We didn't know what was going on" … He will reward everybody for what they did.*

Proverbs 2:7 - *The Lord is a shield to those whose walk is blameless. He guards the path of the just and protects the way of his faithful ones.*

Proverbs 11:13 - *A gossip betrays a confidence, but a trustworthy person keeps a secret.*

Escape Three

(pages 27-36)

Proverbs 3:5, 6 - *Trust in the Lord and do what is right. In everything you do submit to Him and He will keep you on the straight path.*

Proverbs 2:12–15 - *Wisdom will save you from the ways of wicked men, from men whose words are crooked, who have left straight paths to walk in dark places, who get excited in being disobedient and rejoice in doing evil things. Their ways are crooked.*

Proverbs 4:18 - *The path of the righteous is like the morning sun, shining ever brighter till the full light of day.*

Escape Four

(pages 37 - 48)

Proverbs 4:24 - *Keep your mouth free of perversity; keep corrupt talk far from your lips.*

Proverbs 4:6 - *Wisdom will protect you, she will watch over you.*

Proverbs 11:6 - *The goodness of those who live right will save them, the dishonest are trapped by their own desires.*

Proverbs 12:6 - *The words of the wicked are like a deadly ambush, but there is rescue in the words of the upright.*

Proverbs 5:21, 22 – *Your ways are in full view of the Lord. He knows everything you do. Wicked people are trapped by their evil deeds, the ropes of your sins will bind you tight.*

Proverbs 29:25 - *Don't ever be afraid of people, that will become a trap, but if you trust in the Lord you will be safe.*

Escape Five

(pages 49 - 62)

Proverbs 6:9 - *So how long will you lie there, slacker?*

Proverbs 5:3–5 – *The lips of a loose woman drip honey and her speech is smoother than oil but in the end she is bitter as wormwood, like a sharp cut from a double-edged sword. Her feet go down to death; her steps lead straight to the grave.*

Proverbs 5:8–9 - *Stay far away from her, do not go near the door of her house. For your integrity will be stolen by others and your dignity to one who is cruel.*

Proverbs 11:8 - *Good people will be rescued from trouble.*

Proverbs 8:5 - *If you don't know, learn how; if you are stupid, gain some common sense.*

Proverbs 5:15 - *Drink water from your own cistern, find running water in your own well.*

Escape Six

(pages 63 - 78)

Proverbs 6:16–19 - *There are six things the Lord hates, actually seven that are detestable to Him: proud eyes, a lying tongue, hands that shed innocent blood, a heart that makes wicked plans, feet that are quick to rush into evil, a false witness who twists the truth, and a leader who creates conflict in his own country.*

Proverbs 6:9–11 - *When are you going to get up from your sleep? You tell us to let you sleep. You say, just let me snooze a little longer, I need to fold my hands to rest. But then poverty like a robber will take everything from you and all your wealth will be stolen by an armed soldier.*

Proverbs 6:20–22 – *Keep your father's command and don't forsake your mother's teaching. Tie them always to your heart, fasten them around your neck. When you walk, they will guide you; when you sleep they will watch over you; when you wake up they will speak to you.*

Proverbs 6:14–15 - *For those who plot evil with a devious heart and stir up conflict will have disaster overtake them in an instant and be destroyed without anyone to help.*

Proverbs 6:3–5 - *When you are in someone's trap, go to them and in a nice way ask him to release you. If they won't then don't rest until you have been released. Get out like a gazelle escaping from a trap, like a bird flying from a net.*

Proverbs 20:27 – *God's righteousness is his lamp that shines inside us.*

Proverbs 4:18 - *The ways of right-living people glow like a sunrise; the longer they live, the brighter they shine.*

Proverbs 1:23–28 - *Friend, you must change your ways. If you do, I will pour out my wisdom to you, I will make you understand my teachings. But if you refuse to listen when I call and pay no attention when I reach out ... Then you will call to me but I will not answer; You will look for me but will not find me.*

Escape Seven

(pages 79-90)

Proverbs 7:21, 22 - *With persuasive words they can lead you astray. They will seduce you with smooth talk. Those that follow will be like an ox going to be killed, like a deer stepping into a trap.*

Proverbs 4:10–12 - *Take my advice; it will add years to your life. I'm writing out clear directions to the way of wisdom, I'm drawing a map to the right road. I don't want you to end up in a dead end, or waste time making wrong turns.*

Psalm 108:6 - *Save us, mighty God, and help us with your strong right hand, that those you love may be delivered.*

Proverbs 18:10 - *The name of the Lord is a strong fortress; the godly run to him and are safe.*

Proverbs 31:14 – *Like a merchant's ship, bringing food from a long way away.*

Proverbs 15:17 - *A few crusts of bread with someone you love is much better than a feast with someone you hate.*

Escape Eight

(pages 91 - 100)

Proverbs 17:22 - *A cheerful heart is good medicine.*

Proverbs 8:1–9 - *Do you hear Lady Wisdom calling? She is raising her voice. She's taken her stand in the main square, at the busiest intersection. Right in the middle of the city where the traffic is thickest, she shouts, "You—I'm talking to all of you, everyone out here on the streets! Listen, don't be foolish—learn good sense! You dummies—shape up! Don't miss a word of this—I'm telling you how to live well, I'm telling you how to live right."*

Proverbs 30:28 - *It is easy to catch a lizard with your hands, but it still lives in kings' palaces.*

Proverbs 8:1, 2 - *Wisdom is calling us, she has lifted up her voice from the rooftop, from the heights beside the way. Where paths meet, she takes her stand.*

Proverbs 3:23–26 - *You will keep walking safely and your foot will not slip. When you rest, you will not be afraid; when you lie down, your sleep will be sweet. Don't be afraid of sudden fear, or of the wicked ones who are after us. For the LORD will be your confidence and will keep your foot from slipping.*

Escape Nine

(pages 101 - 110)

Proverbs 15:18 – *A hot-tempered person stirs up conflict, but one slow to anger calms everything down.*

Proverbs 25:28 - *A person who does not control his temper is like a city without any defenses.*

Proverbs 9:4–6 – *"Everybody who needs to learn, come and see me!" To people who don't have any sense she says, "Leave your foolish ways and you will live; follow the path that makes sense."*

Proverbs 9:13–18 - *She sits at the door of her house, yelling, "Hey, come and see me! We can steal some good food and drink. No one will ever know!" But those who stop in don't know about those who died listening to her advice.*

Proverbs 9:7–8 - *Whoever argues with a mocker invites insults; whoever rebukes the wicked will be abused. Do not argue with mockers or they will hate you.*

Proverbs 15:12 - *If you argue with a scoffer, all you get is more arguments.*

Escape Ten

(pages 111 - 120)

Proverbs 11:24 – *A person who gives freely gains even more.*

Proverbs 12:24 - *A diligent hand will rule.*

Proverbs 8:19 - *Your fruit is better than solid gold and your harvest is better than silver.*

Proverbs 11:10 - *The whole town celebrates when generous people are successful.*

Proverbs 11:16 – *A kindhearted woman receives honor.*

Proverbs 11:17 - *If you are kind, you will be rewarded, but cruel people only harm themselves.*

Escape Eleven

(pages 121 - 132)

Proverbs 6:6-8 - *Go to the ant, you slacker! Watch its ways and become wise. Without a leader, boss, or ruler, it collects food in summer, gathering provisions during harvest.*

Proverbs 26:14 – *A door swings back and forth on its hinges like a slacker turns over on his bed.*

Proverbs 10:4 - *Lazy hands make you poor, but diligent hands bring riches.*

Proverbs 15:22 – *Where you have no one to guide you, you will fail, but with many instructors you will succeed.*

Proverbs 11:25 - *Whoever brings blessing will be blessed, and one who waters will himself be watered.*

Escape Twelve

(pages 133 - 144)

Proverbs 12:19 - *Truthful lips endure forever, but a lying tongue is but for a moment.*

Proverbs 12:20 - *Deceit is in the heart of those who devise evil, but those who plan peace have joy.*

Proverbs 12:7 - *The wicked will be overthrown and will be no more, but the home of the righteous stands forever.*

Proverbs 12:20, 21 - *Deceit is in the hearts of those who plan evil, but joy is for those who make peace. No harm will overtake the righteous, but for the wicked trouble will never cease.*

Escape Thirteen

(pages 145 - 154)

Proverbs 13:2 – *We will be rewarded as we say good things, even when faithless people only want violence.*

Proverbs 13:19 - *A longing fulfilled will be light and sweetness to your soul.*

Proverbs 13:4 – *If you work hard you will be rewarded.*

Proverbs 13:11 - *If you get things by cheating it will all disappear. But those who build a little at a time will prosper.*

Proverbs 13:24 - *Parents who do not discipline must hate their children, but if they love them they are careful to teach them at all times.*

Proverbs 13:9 – *The lives of good people are a light that shines more brightly every day.*

Proverbs 13:15 - *Sound judgment is praised, but people without good sense are on their way to disaster.*

Proverbs 13:14 - *One who gives wise instruction is like a life-giving fountain, and they will help us to escape all deadly traps.*

Proverbs 13:17 - *A trustworthy messenger brings words of safety.*

Escape Fourteen

(pages 155 - 164)

Proverbs 14:15 - *Silly people will believe anything, but the prudent give careful thought to their steps.*

Proverbs 14:11 - *The house of the wicked will be destroyed, but the tent of the upright will flourish.*

Proverbs 14:17 - *Fools are hotheaded, and quick-tempered people do really foolish things.*

Proverbs 14:1, 2 - *A wise woman builds her house ... She fears the Lord and walks in a prudent way.*

Proverbs 17:22 – *Laughter is as good as medicine.*

Proverbs 14:13 – *Even if your heart aches while you laugh and rejoicing ends in grief.*

Proverbs 14:4 - *Your strong ox no doubt gave you abundant harvest, but where there is no ox the manger is clean.*

Proverbs 14:14 - *Eventually the faithless will be fully repaid for their evil ways and the good rewarded.*

Proverbs 14:22 - *You know those who plot evil will go astray, but those who plan what is good find love and faithfulness.*

Escape Fifteen

(pages 165 - 178)

Proverbs 15:30 - *Light in a messenger's eyes brings joy to the heart, and good news gives health to the bones.*

Proverbs 15:1 - *A gentle answer turns away wrath, but a harsh word stirs up anger.*

Proverbs 15:4 - *A soothing tongue is a tree of life.*

Proverbs 15:13 - *A happy heart makes a cheerful face.*

Proverbs 15:15 - *A cheerful heart has a continual feast.*

Proverbs 1:1–4 - *Proverbs teach you wisdom and instruct you. They help you understand wise sayings. They provide you with instruction and help you live wisely. They lead to what is right and honest and fair. They give understanding to ignorant people. They give knowledge and good sense to those who are young.*

Proverbs 15:33 - *Wisdom will teach you to fear the Lord, and humility comes before honor.*

Proverbs 15:24 - *The path of life leads upward for the prudent, to keep them from going down to the place of the dead.*

Proverbs 15:23 - *...the joy in giving the right answer and know how to give it at the right time.*

Proverbs 15:29 - *The Lord hears the prayers of the righteous.*

Proverbs 15:13 - *Don't let heaviness crush your spirit, a happy heart will always give you a cheerful face.*

Proverbs 14:26 - *The fear of the Lord is a secure fortress, and a safe refuge for the young.*

Proverbs 15:33 - *If I take your correction to heart, I will gain understanding, and wisdom will teach me to fear you, Lord. Now I know that humility comes before honor.*

Summary Outline:

1. **"Wise is better than Strong" (Wisdom)**
Prov. 1:18, 1:33, 9:12, 15:7, 24:5–6

2. **"Right is better than Wrong" (Righteousness)**
Prov. 1:5, 1:10, 2:6, 2:7, 10:28, 11:13, 15:24, 24:11–13

3. **"Straight is better than Crooked" (Integrity)**
Prov. 2:12–13, 3:4–5, 4:18

4. **"Confidence is better than Fear" (Hope)**
Prov. 4:6, 4:24, 5:21–22, 11:6, 12:6, 29:25

5. **"Early is better than Late" (Dependability)**
Prov. 5:3-5, 5:7-9, 5:15, 6:9–11, 8:5, 11:8

6. **"Liberty is better than Bondage" (Freedom)**
Prov. 1:23–28, 4:18, 6:3–5, 6:10–11, 6:14, 6:16–19, 6:20–27

7. **"Safety is better than Danger" (Security)**
Prov. 4:10–12, 7:21–22, 15:17, 18:10, 31:14, Psalm 108:6

8. **"Smart is better than Dumb" (Knowledge)**
Prov. 3:23–25, 8:1–9, 17:22, 20:28

9. **"Glad is better than Mad" (Anger)**
Prov. 9:3–6, 9:7–8, 9:13–18, 15:12, 25:28

10. **"Kind is better than Cruel" (Goodness)**
Prov. 8:19, 11:16–17, 11:24, 12:24

11. **"Work is better than Lazy" (Diligence)**
Prov. 6:6–8, 10:4, 11:25, 15:22, 26:14

12. "Truth is better than Lies" (Honesty)

Prov. 12:7, 12:19–20, 12:21

13. "Light is better than Darkness" (Insight)

Prov. 13 (vv. 2, 4, 11, 14, 15, 17, 19, 24)

14. "Prudent is better than Proud" (Diligence)

Prov. 14 (vv. 1, 2, 4, 11, 13, 15, 17, 22), 17:22

15. "Honor is better than Fame" (Humility)

Prov. 11 (vv. 4 and 33), 14:2, Prov. 15 (vv. 1, 4, 13, 15, 23–24, 29, 30, 33)

Escape! ~ Journal Number Two

The continuing escape tips
by the smartest guy ever.

Escape One

"A Plan is better than Chaos"

The Journal of Henry Gutmann
Captured, imprisoned and scheduled for transport
to Buchenwald prison,
Germany - January 1940

"I hate them! I hate the Nazis! I hate them all. I wish that I had a knife or a gun or a bomb big enough to kill every one of them." Ranting with more anger than Hannah had ever shown, she spewed out as much venom as a fifteen-year-old girl could generate. Certainly more than I had ever seen.

"All of them deserve to die! Every last one of them," Hannah screamed at us in the dank stone room where they had confined us.

My younger brother Hans, standing against the back wall of our prison, looked terrified. "I hope the door is solid enough that they cannot hear you," he whispered with a grimace.

Hannah's heart was bitter. Watching her tears etch crooked tracks in the dirt on her face carved tracks in my own heart. Nothing I could say would help. What could I do? I was only 15 years old. Where were our parents!? Where was my grandfather? We needed Opa to rescue us again.

Sitting on the floor in front of the red-faced Jewish girl we had only known for a few months gave me such a feeling of helplessness, but compassion forced me to reach out and put my hand on her arm. She was the same age as me, she had watched the same horrors and felt the same feelings, but something in my hurting gave me the feeling I needed to reach out. I needed to find a way to help.

Hannah had been forced, with her entire family, onto the death-train cattle car on the way to Buchenwald, a place where Jews by the thousands were being packed into gas chambers and exterminated. Miraculously, Hannah was able to escape. Hans and I had both lost our parents the same way. We did not know if they were dead or alive. All we knew was they had been arrested by the black-uniformed SS, the elite enforcement branch of the Nazi party also called the "Schutzstaffel," and shipped to one of the many prison camps established by Hitler and his murderous soldiers.

The three of us, with the help of my amazing grandfather, Opa, managed to escape the SS. Many times.

Opa—in a desperate attempt to rescue us from the clutches of the Nazis—had successfully evaded capture by our nemesis. As head of the SS in our hometown of Munster, the Commandant had commandeered a frantic chase across Germany as we fled toward the free country of Holland.

We almost made it.

Now all had changed.

Just outside of the town of Enschede, the tanks of the invincible German Panzer Division pinned us down at the border.

Opa was taken captive to be shot as a terrorist spy.

Standing only a few steps from freedom, Opa gave Hans his favorite book from the Scriptures and gave Hannah a set of nesting Russian dolls. My gift was the most precious. He draped his heavy woolen coat over my shoulders, leaving me with the words "Rescue everyone you can."

The hunger to go back and find our parents and free them was great. I looked from Hannah's tear-stained face to my brother's grim clenched jaw and I, Henry Gutmann, knew we had to at least try.

We were grabbed by the SS, imprisoned in the local jail, and were left without food or water while awaiting deportation to the nearest of Hitler's death camps. We were utterly and totally on our own.

(To be continued)

 The Author:

Joe Castillo

I love a good story!

Mexico City was where I was born, grew up and learned to love storytelling and art.

Writing, drawing, illustrating, painting and creating stories in sand for live audiences has filled my life for seven decades. On that journey I almost flunked out of kindergarten, three high schools, Ringling College of Art and Design, Florida Bible College and Asbury Seminary.

Many of the hats I have worn include: advertiser, publisher, pastor, entrepreneur, writer, artist and storyteller. I now wear a beret, and I wrote this story for you.

My "storytelling artwork" was born out of a struggle to forgive, which I wrote about in my first book, *The Face of Christ*. SandStory has been my greatest adventure in Storytelling. I use sand, light and music to engage and inspire audiences all over the world.

These 'SandStories' have been performed in over twenty countries for churches, conferences, Fortune 500 companies, world leaders, CBS, NBC, the BBC and reached the finals on America's Got Talent.

My "Glad Girl" Cindy and I have four kids, eight grandkids and love living just south of Atlanta, Georgia in a new town for creatives called Trilith.

If you are nearby, stop and visit. Contact me through JoeCastillo.com or SandStory.com

Books by

Joe Castillo

- *The Face of Christ: A Story of Loss, Forgiveness, and Restoration*
- *SandStory: How Ordinary Sand Changed My Life*
- *Love Letters: A Study Guide of Psalm 119*
- *Love Letters: Search with All Your Heart* (**for young women**)
- *Escape! Snares, Traps, and How to Escape!* (**for boys**)

Find Joe Castillo's books at JoeCastillo.com or wherever fine books are sold.

The Book of Proverbs

CHAPTERS 1–15
FREE BIBLE VERSION

Chapter 1 - Wise is better than Strong (Wisdom)

1 The proverbs of Solomon son of David, king of Israel:

2 for gaining wisdom and instruction;
   for understanding words of insight;

3 for receiving instruction in prudent behavior,
   doing what is right and just and fair;

4 for giving prudence to those who are simple,
   knowledge and discretion to the young—

5 let the wise listen and add to their learning,
   and let the discerning get guidance—

6 for understanding proverbs and parables,
   the sayings and riddles of the wise.

7 The fear of the Lord is the beginning of knowledge,
   but fools despise wisdom and instruction.

8 Listen, my son, to your father's instruction
   and do not forsake your mother's teaching.

9 They are a garland to grace your head
   and a chain to adorn your neck.

10 My son, if sinful men entice you,
   do not give in to them.

11 If they say, "Come along with us;
  let's lie in wait for innocent blood,
  let's ambush some harmless soul;
12 let's swallow them alive, like the grave,
  and whole, like those who go down to the pit;
13 we will get all sorts of valuable things
  and fill our houses with plunder;
14 cast lots with us;
  we will all share the loot"—
15 my son, do not go along with them,
  do not set foot on their paths;
16 for their feet rush into evil,
  they are swift to shed blood.
17 How useless to spread a net
  where every bird can see it!
18 These men lie in wait for their own blood;
  they ambush only themselves!
19 Such are the paths of all who go after ill-gotten gain;
  it takes away the life of those who get it.
20 Out in the open wisdom calls aloud,
  she raises her voice in the public square;
21 on top of the wall she cries out,
  at the city gate she makes her speech:
22 "How long will you who are simple love your simple ways?
  How long will mockers delight in mockery
  and fools hate knowledge?

23 Repent at my rebuke!
　　Then I will pour out my thoughts to you,
　　I will make known to you my teachings.
24 But since you refuse to listen when I call
　　and no one pays attention when I stretch out my hand,
25 since you disregard all my advice
　　and do not accept my rebuke,
26 I in turn will laugh when disaster strikes you;
　　I will mock when calamity overtakes you—
27 when calamity overtakes you like a storm,
　　when disaster sweeps over you like a whirlwind,
　　when distress and trouble overwhelm you.
28 "Then they will call to me but I will not answer;
　　they will look for me but will not find me,
29 since they hated knowledge
　　and did not choose to fear the Lord.
30 Since they would not accept my advice
　　and spurned my rebuke,
31 they will eat the fruit of their ways
　　and be filled with the fruit of their schemes.
32 For the waywardness of the simple will kill them,
　　and the complacency of fools will destroy them;
33 but whoever listens to me will live in safety
　　and be at ease, without fear of harm."

Chapter 2 - Right is better than Wrong (Righteousness)

1 My son, if you accept my words
  and store up my commands within you,

2 turning your ear to wisdom
  and applying your heart to understanding—

3 indeed, if you call out for insight
  and cry aloud for understanding,

4 and if you look for it as for silver
  and search for it as for hidden treasure,

5 then you will understand the fear of the Lord
  and find the knowledge of God.

6 For the Lord gives wisdom;
  from his mouth come knowledge and understanding.

7 He holds success in store for the upright,
  he is a shield to those whose walk is blameless,

8 for he guards the course of the just
  and protects the way of his faithful ones.

9 Then you will understand what is right and just
  and fair—every good path.

10 For wisdom will enter your heart,
  and knowledge will be pleasant to your soul.

11 Discretion will protect you,
  and understanding will guard you.

12 Wisdom will save you from the ways of wicked men,
  from men whose words are perverse,

13 who have left the straight paths
  to walk in dark ways,

14 who delight in doing wrong
  and rejoice in the perverseness of evil,

15 whose paths are crooked
  and who are devious in their ways.

16 Wisdom will save you also from the adulterous woman,
  from the wayward woman with her seductive words,

17 who has left the partner of her youth
  and ignored the covenant she made before God.

18 Surely her house leads down to death
  and her paths to the spirits of the dead.

19 None who go to her return
  or attain the paths of life.

20 Thus you will walk in the ways of the good
  and keep to the paths of the righteous.

21 For the upright will live in the land,
  and the blameless will remain in it;

22 but the wicked will be cut off from the land,
  and the unfaithful will be torn from it.

Chapter 3 - Straight is better than Crooked (Integrity)

1 My son, do not forget my teaching,
  but keep my commands in your heart,

2 for they will prolong your life many years
  and bring you peace and prosperity.

3 Let love and faithfulness never leave you;
  bind them around your neck,
  write them on the tablet of your heart.

4 Then you will win favor and a good name
   in the sight of God and man.
5 Trust in the Lord with all your heart
   and lean not on your own understanding;
6 in all your ways submit to him,
   and he will make your paths straight.
7 Do not be wise in your own eyes;
   fear the Lord and shun evil.
8 This will bring health to your body
   and nourishment to your bones.
9 Honor the Lord with your wealth,
   with the first fruits of all your crops;
10 then your barns will be filled to overflowing,
   and your vats will brim over with new wine.
11 My son, do not despise the Lord's discipline,
   and do not resent his rebuke,
12 because the Lord disciplines those he loves,
   as a father the son he delights in.
13 Blessed are those who find wisdom,
   those who gain understanding,
14 for she is more profitable than silver
   and yields better returns than gold.
15 She is more precious than rubies;
   nothing you desire can compare with her.
16 Long life is in her right hand;
   in her left hand are riches and honor.
17 Her ways are pleasant ways,
   and all her paths are peace.

18 She is a tree of life to those who take hold of her;
  those who hold her fast will be blessed.

19 By wisdom the Lord laid the earth's foundations,
  by understanding he set the heavens in place;

20 by his knowledge the watery depths were divided,
  and the clouds let drop the dew.

21 My son, do not let wisdom and understanding out of your sight,
  preserve sound judgment and discretion;

22 they will be life for you,
  an ornament to grace your neck.

23 Then you will go on your way in safety,
  and your foot will not stumble.

24 When you lie down, you will not be afraid;
  when you lie down, your sleep will be sweet.

25 Have no fear of sudden disaster
  or of the ruin that overtakes the wicked,

26 for the Lord will be at your side
  and will keep your foot from being snared.

27 Do not withhold good from those to whom it is due,
  when it is in your power to act.

28 Do not say to your neighbor,
  "Come back tomorrow and I'll give it to you"—
  when you already have it with you.

29 Do not plot harm against your neighbor,
  who lives trustfully near you.

30 Do not accuse anyone for no reason—
  when they have done you no harm.

31 Do not envy the violent
   or choose any of their ways.
32 For the Lord detests the perverse
   but takes the upright into his confidence.
33 The Lord's curse is on the house of the wicked,
   but he blesses the home of the righteous.
34 He mocks proud mockers
   but shows favor to the humble and oppressed.
35 The wise inherit honor,
   but fools get only shame.

Chapter 4 - Confidence is getter than Fear (Hope)

1 Listen, my sons, to a father's instruction;
   pay attention and gain understanding.
2 I give you sound learning,
   so do not forsake my teaching.
3 For I too was a son to my father,
   still tender, and cherished by my mother.
4 Then he taught me, and he said to me,
   "Take hold of my words with all your heart;
   keep my commands, and you will live.
5 Get wisdom, get understanding;
   do not forget my words or turn away from them.
6 Do not forsake wisdom, and she will protect you;
   love her, and she will watch over you.
7 The beginning of wisdom is this: Get wisdom.
   Though it cost all you have, get understanding.

8 Cherish her, and she will exalt you;

  embrace her, and she will honor you.

9 She will give you a garland to grace your head

  and present you with a glorious crown."

10 Listen, my son, accept what I say,

  and the years of your life will be many.

11 I instruct you in the way of wisdom

  and lead you along straight paths.

12 When you walk, your steps will not be hampered;

  when you run, you will not stumble.

13 Hold on to instruction, do not let it go;

  guard it well, for it is your life.

14 Do not set foot on the path of the wicked

  or walk in the way of evildoers.

15 Avoid it, do not travel on it;

  turn from it and go on your way.

16 For they cannot rest until they do evil;

  they are robbed of sleep till they make someone stumble.

17 They eat the bread of wickedness

  and drink the wine of violence.

18 The path of the righteous is like the morning sun,

  shining ever brighter till the full light of day.

19 But the way of the wicked is like deep darkness;

  they do not know what makes them stumble.

20 My son, pay attention to what I say;

  turn your ear to my words.

21 Do not let them out of your sight,

  keep them within your heart;

22 for they are life to those who find them

and health to one's whole body.

23 Above all else, guard your heart,

for everything you do flows from it.

24 Keep your mouth free of perversity;

keep corrupt talk far from your lips.

25 Let your eyes look straight ahead;

fix your gaze directly before you.

26 Give careful thought to the paths for your feet

and be steadfast in all your ways.

27 Do not turn to the right or the left;

keep your foot from evil.

Chapter 5 - Early is better than Late (Dependability)

1 My son, pay attention to my wisdom,

turn your ear to my words of insight,

2 that you may maintain discretion

and your lips may preserve knowledge.

3 For the lips of the adulterous woman drip honey,

and her speech is smoother than oil;

4 but in the end she is bitter as gall,

sharp as a double-edged sword.

5 Her feet go down to death;

her steps lead straight to the grave.

6 She gives no thought to the way of life;

her paths wander aimlessly, but she does not know it.

7 Now then, my sons, listen to me;
do not turn aside from what I say.

8 Keep to a path far from her,
do not go near the door of her house,

9 lest you lose your honor to others
and your dignity to one who is cruel,

10 lest strangers feast on your wealth
and your toil enrich the house of another.

11 At the end of your life you will groan,
when your flesh and body are spent.

12 You will say, "How I hated discipline!
How my heart spurned correction!

13 I would not obey my teachers
or turn my ear to my instructors.

14 And I was soon in serious trouble
in the assembly of God's people."

15 Drink water from your own cistern,
running water from your own well.

16 Should your springs overflow in the streets,
your streams of water in the public squares?

17 Let them be yours alone,
never to be shared with strangers.

18 May your fountain be blessed,
and may you rejoice in the wife of your youth.

19 A loving doe, a graceful deer—
may her breasts satisfy you always,
may you ever be intoxicated with her love.

20 Why, my son, be intoxicated with another man's wife?

Why embrace the bosom of a wayward woman?

21 For your ways are in full view of the Lord,

and he examines all your paths.

22 The evil deeds of the wicked ensnare them;

the cords of their sins hold them fast.

23 For lack of discipline they will die,

led astray by their own great folly.

Chapter 6 - Liberty is better than Bondage (Freedom)

1 My son, if you have put up security for your neighbor,

if you have shaken hands in pledge for a stranger,

2 you have been trapped by what you said,

ensnared by the words of your mouth.

3 So do this, my son, to free yourself,

since you have fallen into your neighbor's hands:

Go—to the point of exhaustion—

and give your neighbor no rest!

4 Allow no sleep to your eyes,

no slumber to your eyelids.

5 Free yourself, like a gazelle from the hand of the hunter,

like a bird from the snare of the fowler.

6 Go to the ant, you sluggard;

consider its ways and be wise!

7 It has no commander,

no overseer or ruler,

8 yet it stores its provisions in summer
  and gathers its food at harvest.

9 How long will you lie there, you sluggard?
  When will you get up from your sleep?

10 A little sleep, a little slumber,
  a little folding of the hands to rest—

11 and poverty will come on you like a thief
  and scarcity like an armed man.

12 A troublemaker and a villain,
  who goes about with a corrupt mouth,

13   who winks maliciously with his eye,
  signals with his feet
  and motions with his fingers,

14   who plots evil with deceit in his heart—
  he always stirs up conflict.

15 Therefore disaster will overtake him in an instant;
  he will suddenly be destroyed—without remedy.

16 There are six things the Lord hates,
  seven that are detestable to him:

17   - Haughty eyes,
  - A lying tongue,
  - Hands that shed innocent blood,

18   - A heart that devises wicked schemes,
  - Feet that are quick to rush into evil,

19   - A false witness who pours out lies,
  - A person who stirs up conflict in the community.

20 My son, keep your father's command
  and do not forsake your mother's teaching.

21 Bind them always on your heart;

   fasten them around your neck.

22 When you walk, they will guide you;

   when you sleep, they will watch over you;

   when you awake, they will speak to you.

23 For this command is a lamp, this teaching is a light,

      and correction and instruction are the way to life,

24 keeping you from your neighbor's wife,

   from the smooth talk of a wayward woman.

25 Do not lust in your heart after her beauty

   or let her captivate you with her eyes.

26 For a prostitute can be had for a loaf of bread,

   but another man's wife preys on your very life.

27 Can a man scoop fire into his lap

   without his clothes being burned?

28 Can a man walk on hot coals

   without his feet being scorched?

29 So is he who sleeps with another man's wife;

   no one who touches her will go unpunished.

30 People do not despise a thief if he steals

   to satisfy his hunger when he is starving.

31 Yet if he is caught, he must pay sevenfold,

   though it costs him all the wealth of his house.

32 But a man who commits adultery has no sense;

   whoever does so destroys himself.

33 Blows and disgrace are his lot,

   and his shame will never be wiped away.

34 For jealousy arouses a husband's fury,

    and he will show no mercy when he takes revenge.

35 He will not accept any compensation;

    he will refuse a bribe, however great it is.

Chapter 7 - Safety is better than Danger (Security)

1 My son, keep my words

    and store up my commands within you.

2 Keep my commands and you will live;

    guard my teachings as the apple of your eye.

3 Bind them on your fingers;

    write them on the tablet of your heart.

4 Say to wisdom, "You are my sister,"

    and to insight, "You are my relative."

5 They will keep you from the adulterous woman,

    from the wayward woman with her seductive words.

6 At the window of my house

    I looked down through the lattice.

7 I saw among the simple,

    I noticed among the young men,

    a youth who had no sense.

8 He was going down the street near her corner,

    walking along in the direction of her house

9 at twilight, as the day was fading,

    as the dark of night set in.

10 Then out came a woman to meet him,

    dressed like a prostitute and with crafty intent.

11 (She is unruly and defiant,

her feet never stay at home;

12 now in the street, now in the squares,

at every corner she lurks.)

13 She took hold of him and kissed him

and with a brazen face she said:

14 "Today I fulfilled my vows,

and I have food from my fellowship offering at home.

15 So I came out to meet you;

I looked for you and have found you!

16 I have covered my bed

with colored linens from Egypt.

17 I have perfumed my bed

with myrrh, aloes and cinnamon.

18 Come, let's drink deeply of love till morning;

let's enjoy ourselves with love!

19 My husband is not at home;

he has gone on a long journey.

20 He took his purse filled with money

and will not be home till full moon."

21 With persuasive words she led him astray;

she seduced him with her smooth talk.

22 All at once he followed her

like an ox going to the slaughter,

like a deer stepping into a noose

23 till an arrow pierces his liver,

like a bird darting into a snare,

little knowing it will cost him his life.

24 Now then, my sons, listen to me;
   pay attention to what I say.

25 Do not let your heart turn to her ways
   or stray into her paths.

26 Many are the victims she has brought down;
   her slain are a mighty throng.

27 Her house is a highway to the grave,
   leading down to the chambers of death.

Chapter 8 - Smart is better than Dumb (Knowledge)

1 Does not wisdom call out?
   Does not understanding raise her voice?

2 At the highest point along the way,
   where the paths meet, she takes her stand;

3 beside the gate leading into the city,
   at the entrance, she cries aloud:

4 "To you, O people, I call out;
   I raise my voice to all mankind.

5 You who are simple, gain prudence;
   you who are foolish, set your hearts on it.

6 Listen, for I have trustworthy things to say;
   I open my lips to speak what is right.

7 My mouth speaks what is true,
   for my lips detest wickedness.

8 All the words of my mouth are just;
   none of them is crooked or perverse.

9 To the discerning all of them are right;

they are upright to those who have found knowledge.

10 Choose my instruction instead of silver,

knowledge rather than choice gold,

11 for wisdom is more precious than rubies,

and nothing you desire can compare with her.

12 "I, wisdom, dwell together with prudence;

I possess knowledge and discretion.

13 To fear the Lord is to hate evil;

I hate pride and arrogance,

evil behavior and perverse speech.

14 Counsel and sound judgment are mine;

I have insight, I have power.

15 By me kings reign

and rulers issue decrees that are just;

16 by me princes govern,

and nobles—all who rule on earth.

17 I love those who love me,

and those who seek me find me.

18 With me are riches and honor,

enduring wealth and prosperity.

19 My fruit is better than fine gold;

what I yield surpasses choice silver.

20 I walk in the way of righteousness,

along the paths of justice,

21 bestowing a rich inheritance on those who love me

and making their treasuries full.

22 "The Lord brought me forth as the first of his works,
   before his deeds of old;
23 I was formed long ages ago,
   at the very beginning, when the world came to be.
24 When there were no watery depths, I was given birth,
   when there were no springs overflowing with water;
25 before the mountains were settled in place,
   before the hills, I was given birth,
26 before he made the world or its fields
   or any of the dust of the earth.
27 I was there when he set the heavens in place,
   when he marked out the horizon on the face of the deep,
28 when he established the clouds above
   and fixed securely the fountains of the deep,
29 when he gave the sea its boundary
       so the waters would not overstep his command,
       and when he marked out the foundations of the
earth.
30 Then I was constantly at his side.
       I was filled with delight day after day, rejoicing always
in his presence,
31 rejoicing in his whole world
   and delighting in mankind.
32 "Now then, my children, listen to me;
   blessed are those who keep my ways.
33 Listen to my instruction and be wise;
   do not disregard it.

34 Blessed are those who listen to me,
  watching daily at my doors,
  waiting at my doorway.
35 For those who find me find life
  and receive favor from the Lord.
36 But those who fail to find me harm themselves;
  all who hate me love death."

Chapter 9 - Glad is better than Mad (Gratitude)

1 Wisdom has built her house;
  she has set up its seven pillars.
2 She has prepared her meat and mixed her wine;
  she has also set her table.
3 She has sent out her servants, and she calls
  from the highest point of the city,
4 "Let all who are simple come to my house!"
  To those who have no sense she says,
5 "Come, eat my food
  and drink the wine I have mixed.
6 Leave your simple ways and you will live;
  walk in the way of insight."
7 Whoever corrects a mocker invites insults;
  whoever rebukes the wicked incurs abuse.
8 Do not rebuke mockers or they will hate you;
  rebuke the wise and they will love you.
9 Instruct the wise and they will be wiser still;
  teach the righteous and they will add to their learning.

10 The fear of the Lord is the beginning of wisdom,
and knowledge of the Holy One is understanding.

11 For through wisdom your days will be many,
and years will be added to your life.

12 If you are wise, your wisdom will reward you;
if you are a mocker, you alone will suffer.

13 Folly is an unruly woman;
she is simple and knows nothing.

14 She sits at the door of her house,
on a seat at the highest point of the city,

15 calling out to those who pass by,
who go straight on their way,

16 "Let all who are simple come to my house!"
To those who have no sense she says,

17 "Stolen water is sweet;
food eaten in secret is delicious!"

18 But little do they know that the dead are there,
that her guests are deep in the realm of the dead.

Chapter 10 - Kind is better than Cruel (Goodness)

1 A wise son brings joy to his father,
but a foolish son brings grief to his mother.

2 Ill-gotten treasures have no lasting value,
but righteousness delivers from death.

3 The Lord does not let the righteous go hungry,
but he thwarts the craving of the wicked.

4 Lazy hands make for poverty,

but diligent hands bring wealth.

5 He who gathers crops in summer is a prudent son,

but he who sleeps during harvest is a disgraceful son.

6 Blessings crown the head of the righteous,

but violence overwhelms the mouth of the wicked.

7 The name of the righteous is used in blessings,

but the name of the wicked will rot.

8 The wise in heart accept commands,

but a chattering fool comes to ruin.

9 Whoever walks in integrity walks securely,

but whoever takes crooked paths will be found out.

10 Whoever winks maliciously causes grief,

and a chattering fool comes to ruin.

11 The mouth of the righteous is a fountain of life,

but the mouth of the wicked conceals violence.

12 Hatred stirs up conflict,

but love covers over all wrongs.

13 Wisdom is found on the lips of the discerning,

but a rod is for the back of one who has no sense.

14 The wise store up knowledge,

but the mouth of a fool invites ruin.

15 The wealth of the rich is their fortified city,

but poverty is the ruin of the poor.

16 The wages of the righteous is life,

but the earnings of the wicked are sin and death.

17 Whoever heeds discipline shows the way to life,

but whoever ignores correction leads others astray.

18 Whoever conceals hatred with lying lips
   and spreads slander is a fool.
19 Sin is not ended by multiplying words,
   but the prudent hold their tongues.
20 The tongue of the righteous is choice silver,
   but the heart of the wicked is of little value.
21 The lips of the righteous nourish many,
   but fools die for lack of sense.
22 The blessing of the Lord brings wealth,
   without painful toil for it.
23 A fool finds pleasure in wicked schemes,
   but a person of understanding delights in wisdom.
24 What the wicked dread will overtake them;
   what the righteous desire will be granted.
25 When the storm has swept by, the wicked are gone,
   but the righteous stand firm forever.
26 As vinegar to the teeth and smoke to the eyes,
   so are sluggards to those who send them.
27 The fear of the Lord adds length to life,
   but the years of the wicked are cut short.
28 The prospect of the righteous is joy,
   but the hopes of the wicked come to nothing.
29 The way of the Lord is a refuge for the blameless,
   but it is the ruin of those who do evil.
30 The righteous will never be uprooted,
   but the wicked will not remain in the land.

31 From the mouth of the righteous comes the fruit of wisdom,

but a perverse tongue will be silenced.

32 The lips of the righteous know what finds favor,

but the mouth of the wicked only what is perverse.

Chapter 11 - Work is better than Lazy (Diligence)

1 The Lord detests dishonest scales,

but accurate weights find favor with him.

2 When pride comes, then comes disgrace,

but with humility comes wisdom.

3 The integrity of the upright guides them,

but the unfaithful are destroyed by their duplicity.

4 Wealth is worthless in the day of wrath,

but righteousness delivers from death.

5 The righteousness of the blameless makes their paths straight,

but the wicked are brought down by their own wickedness.

6 The righteousness of the upright delivers them,

but the unfaithful are trapped by evil desires.

7 Hopes placed in mortals die with them;

all the promise of their power comes to nothing.

8 The righteous person is rescued from trouble,

and it falls on the wicked instead.

9 With their mouths the godless destroy their neighbors,

but through knowledge the righteous escape.

10 When the righteous prosper, the city rejoices;

when the wicked perish, there are shouts of joy.

11 Through the blessing of the upright a city is exalted,

but by the mouth of the wicked it is destroyed.

12 Whoever derides their neighbor has no sense,

but the one who has understanding holds their tongue.

13 A gossip betrays a confidence,

but a trustworthy person keeps a secret.

14 For lack of guidance a nation falls,

but victory is won through many advisers.

15 Whoever puts up security for a stranger will surely suffer,

but whoever refuses to shake hands in pledge is safe.

16 A kindhearted woman gains honor,

but ruthless men gain only wealth.

17 Those who are kind benefit themselves,

but the cruel bring ruin on themselves.

18 A wicked person earns deceptive wages,

but the one who sows righteousness reaps a sure reward.

19 Truly the righteous attain life,

but whoever pursues evil finds death.

20 The Lord detests those whose hearts are perverse,

but he delights in those whose ways are blameless.

21 Be sure of this: The wicked will not go unpunished,

but those who are righteous will go free.

22 Like a gold ring in a pig's snout

is a beautiful woman who shows no discretion.

23 The desire of the righteous ends only in good,

but the hope of the wicked only in wrath.

24 One person gives freely, yet gains even more;

another withholds unduly, but comes to poverty.

25 A generous person will prosper;

whoever refreshes others will be refreshed.

26 People curse the one who hoards grain,

but they pray God's blessing on the one who is willing to sell.

27 Whoever seeks good finds favor,

but evil comes to one who searches for it.

28 Those who trust in their riches will fall,

but the righteous will thrive like a green leaf.

29 Whoever brings ruin on their family will inherit only wind,

and the fool will be servant to the wise.

30 The fruit of the righteous is a tree of life,

and the one who is wise saves lives.

31 If the righteous receive their due on earth,

how much more the ungodly and the sinner!

Chapter 12 - Truth is better than Lies (Honesty)

1 Whoever loves discipline loves knowledge,

but whoever hates correction is stupid.

2 Good people obtain favor from the Lord,

but he condemns those who devise wicked schemes.

3 No one can be established through wickedness,

but the righteous cannot be uprooted.

4 A wife of noble character is her husband's crown,

but a disgraceful wife is like decay in his bones.

5 The plans of the righteous are just,
   but the advice of the wicked is deceitful.
6 The words of the wicked lie in wait for blood,
   but the speech of the upright rescues them.
7 The wicked are overthrown and are no more,
   but the house of the righteous stands firm.
8 A person is praised according to their prudence,
   and one with a warped mind is despised.
9 Better to be a nobody and yet have a servant
   than pretend to be somebody and have no food.
10 The righteous care for the needs of their animals,
   but the kindest acts of the wicked are cruel.
11 Those who work their land will have abundant food,
   but those who chase fantasies have no sense.
12 The wicked desire the stronghold of evildoers,
   but the root of the righteous endures.
13 Evildoers are trapped by their sinful talk,
   and so the innocent escape trouble.
14 From the fruit of their lips people are filled with good things,
   and the work of their hands brings them reward.
15 The way of fools seems right to them,
   but the wise listen to advice.
16 Fools show their annoyance at once,
   but the prudent overlook an insult.
17 An honest witness tells the truth,
   but a false witness tells lies.

18 The words of the reckless pierce like swords,
   but the tongue of the wise brings healing.

19 Truthful lips endure forever,
   but a lying tongue lasts only a moment.

20 Deceit is in the hearts of those who plot evil,
   but those who promote peace have joy.

21 No harm overtakes the righteous,
   but the wicked have their fill of trouble.

22 The Lord detests lying lips,
   but he delights in people who are trustworthy.

23 The prudent keep their knowledge to themselves,
   but a fool's heart blurts out folly.

24 Diligent hands will rule,
   but laziness ends in forced labor.

25 Anxiety weighs down the heart,
   but a kind word cheers it up.

26 The righteous choose their friends carefully,
   but the way of the wicked leads them astray.

27 The lazy do not roast any game,
   but the diligent feed on the riches of the hunt.

28 In the way of righteousness there is life;
   along that path is immortality.

Chapter 13 - *Light is better than Darkness (Insight)*

1 A wise son heeds his father's instruction,
   but a mocker does not respond to rebukes.

2 From the fruit of their lips people enjoy good things,
    but the unfaithful have an appetite for violence.

3 Those who guard their lips preserve their lives,
    but those who speak rashly will come to ruin.

4 A sluggard's appetite is never filled,
    but the desires of the diligent are fully satisfied.

5 The righteous hate what is false,
    but the wicked make themselves a stench
    and bring shame on themselves.

6 Righteousness guards the person of integrity,
    but wickedness overthrows the sinner.

7 One person pretends to be rich, yet has nothing;
    another pretends to be poor, yet has great wealth.

8 A person's riches may ransom their life,
    but the poor cannot respond to threatening rebukes.

9 The light of the righteous shines brightly,
    but the lamp of the wicked is snuffed out.

10 Where there is strife, there is pride,
    but wisdom is found in those who take advice.

11 Dishonest money dwindles away,
    but whoever gathers money little by little makes it grow.

12 Hope deferred makes the heart sick,
    but a longing fulfilled is a tree of life.

13 Whoever scorns instruction will pay for it,
    but whoever respects a command is rewarded.

14 The teaching of the wise is a fountain of life,
    turning a person from the snares of death.

15 Good judgment wins favor,

but the way of the unfaithful leads to their destruction.

16 All who are prudent act with knowledge,

but fools expose their folly.

17 A wicked messenger falls into trouble,

but a trustworthy envoy brings healing.

18 Whoever disregards discipline comes to poverty and shame,

but whoever heeds correction is honored.

19 A longing fulfilled is sweet to the soul,

but fools detest turning from evil.

20 Walk with the wise and become wise,

for a companion of fools suffers harm.

21 Trouble pursues the sinner,

but the righteous are rewarded with good things.

22 A good person leaves an inheritance for their children's children,

but a sinner's wealth is stored up for the righteous.

23 An unplowed field produces food for the poor,

but injustice sweeps it away.

24 Whoever spares the rod hates their children,

but the one who loves their children is careful to discipline them.

25 The righteous eat to their hearts' content,

but the stomach of the wicked goes hungry.

Chapter 14 - Prudent is better than Proud (Discernment)

1 The wise woman builds her house,
   but with her own hands the foolish one tears hers down.

2 Whoever fears the Lord walks uprightly,
   but those who despise him are devious in their ways.

3 A fool's mouth lashes out with pride,
   but the lips of the wise protect them.

4 Where there are no oxen, the manger is empty,
   but from the strength of an ox come abundant harvests.

5 An honest witness does not deceive,
   but a false witness pours out lies.

6 The mocker seeks wisdom and finds none,
   but knowledge comes easily to the discerning.

7 Stay away from a fool,
   for you will not find knowledge on their lips.

8 The wisdom of the prudent is to give thought to their ways,
   but the folly of fools is deception.

9 Fools mock at making amends for sin,
   but goodwill is found among the upright.

10 Each heart knows its own bitterness,
   and no one else can share its joy.

11 The house of the wicked will be destroyed,
   but the tent of the upright will flourish.

12 There is a way that appears to be right,
   but in the end it leads to death.

13 Even in laughter the heart may ache,

and rejoicing may end in grief.

14 The faithless will be fully repaid for their ways,

and the good rewarded for theirs.

15 The simple believe anything,

but the prudent give thought to their steps.

16 The wise fear the Lord and shun evil,

but a fool is hotheaded and yet feels secure.

17 A quick-tempered person does foolish things,

and the one who devises evil schemes is hated.

18 The simple inherit folly,

but the prudent are crowned with knowledge.

19 Evildoers will bow down in the presence of the good,

and the wicked at the gates of the righteous.

20 The poor are shunned even by their neighbors,

but the rich have many friends.

21 It is a sin to despise one's neighbor,

but blessed is the one who is kind to the needy.

22 Do not those who plot evil go astray?

But those who plan what is good find love and faithfulness.

23 All hard work brings a profit,

but mere talk leads only to poverty.

24 The wealth of the wise is their crown,

but the folly of fools yields folly.

25 A truthful witness saves lives,

but a false witness is deceitful.

26 Whoever fears the Lord has a secure fortress,

and for their children it will be a refuge.

27 The fear of the Lord is a fountain of life,
   turning a person from the snares of death.

28 A large population is a king's glory,
   but without subjects a prince is ruined.

29 Whoever is patient has great understanding,
   but one who is quick-tempered displays folly.

30 A heart at peace gives life to the body,
   but envy rots the bones.

31 Whoever oppresses the poor shows contempt for their Maker,
   but whoever is kind to the needy honors God.

32 When calamity comes, the wicked are brought down,
   but even in death the righteous seek refuge in God.

33 Wisdom reposes in the heart of the discerning
   and even among fools she lets herself be known.

34 Righteousness exalts a nation,
   but sin condemns any people.

35 A king delights in a wise servant,
   but a shameful servant arouses his fury.

Chapter 15 - Honor is better than Fame (Humility)

1 A gentle answer turns away wrath,
   but a harsh word stirs up anger.

2 The tongue of the wise adorns knowledge,
   but the mouth of the fool gushes folly.

3 The eyes of the Lord are everywhere,
   keeping watch on the wicked and the good.

4 The soothing tongue is a tree of life,

but a perverse tongue crushes the spirit.

5 A fool spurns a parent's discipline,

but whoever heeds correction shows prudence.

6 The house of the righteous contains great treasure,

but the income of the wicked brings ruin.

7 The lips of the wise spread knowledge,

but the hearts of fools are not upright.

8 The Lord detests the sacrifice of the wicked,

but the prayer of the upright pleases him.

9 The Lord detests the way of the wicked,

but he loves those who pursue righteousness.

10 Stern discipline awaits anyone who leaves the path;

the one who hates correction will die.

11 Death and Destruction lie open before the Lord—

how much more do human hearts!

12 Mockers resent correction,

so they avoid the wise.

13 A happy heart makes the face cheerful,

but heartache crushes the spirit.

14 The discerning heart seeks knowledge,

but the mouth of a fool feeds on folly.

15 All the days of the oppressed are wretched,

but the cheerful heart has a continual feast.

16 Better a little with the fear of the Lord

than great wealth with turmoil.

17 Better a small serving of vegetables with love

than a fattened calf with hatred.

18 A hot-tempered person stirs up conflict,
   but the one who is patient calms a quarrel.

19 The way of the sluggard is blocked with thorns,
   but the path of the upright is a highway.

20 A wise son brings joy to his father,
   but a foolish man despises his mother.

21 Folly brings joy to one who has no sense,
   but whoever has understanding keeps a straight course.

22 Plans fail for lack of counsel,
   but with many advisers they succeed.

23 A person finds joy in giving an apt reply—
   and how good is a timely word!

24 The path of life leads upward for the prudent
   to keep them from going down to the realm of the dead.

25 The Lord tears down the house of the proud,
   but he sets the widow's boundary stones in place.

26 The Lord detests the thoughts of the wicked,
   but gracious words are pure in his sight.

27 The greedy bring ruin to their households,
   but the one who hates bribes will live.

28 The heart of the righteous weighs its answers,
   but the mouth of the wicked gushes evil.

29 The Lord is far from the wicked,
   but he hears the prayer of the righteous.

30 Light in a messenger's eyes brings joy to the heart,
   and good news gives health to the bones.

31 Whoever heeds life-giving correction
   will be at home among the wise.

32 Those who disregard discipline despise themselves,
   but the one who heeds correction gains understanding.
33 Wisdom's instruction is to fear the Lord,
   and humility comes before honor.